WOMEN OF THE CATARACT

Merlene Fawdry

Fixwrite

First published Fixwrite 2017
© Merlene Fawdry 2017
mfawdry@bigpond.net.au
ISBN: 978-0-9954333-0-4:

National Library of Australia Cataloguing-in-Publication entry
Creator: Fawdry, Merlene, 1946- author.
Title: Women of the Cataract / Merlene Fawdry.
Edition: 1st edition.
ISBN: 9780995433304 (paperback)

Subjects: Authors--Tasmania--Launceston--Fiction.

Cyberstalking--Tasmania--Launceston--Fiction.

Spirits--Tasmania--Launceston--Fiction.

Ghost stories.

Paranormal fiction.

Launceston (Tas.)--Fiction.

Cover design by End2End Books

This book is dedicated to older writers whose formal education ended early due to the expectations of society, economics of a past era, and the responsibilities of life, their dream of writing deferred until families gained adult independence, alternative careers ended, and retirement gave them the time and space to write and who, through dedication and persistence, contribute to age diversity in writing.

Prologue

I returned to the cottage after my husband's death. It held memories of happier times and offered a roof over my head. My son had worked alongside his father since he was a small boy and knew how to care for the place better than any grown man. He needed to, because the cottage went with the groundkeeper's position to which he had been appointed. My work as a woman didn't count, even though I was out in all weathers at the toll gate, all too often dealing with those intent on mischief, the inebriated and the dishonest. It had all been in a day's work for me until fate bestowed another, more important, task for me to undertake and the deliverance of the women and children of the cataract was in my hands.

Martha Boyd

Chapter 1

Houses, like people, hold fast to the confidences of those who have gone before, until those secrets become the essence of the building. In the end they permeate every crevice of the structure, leaving only the benign façade as a sleight of hand invitation to the unsuspecting.

The Tollkeeper's Cottage held a fascination for me from the first time I saw it, crossing the bridge on the way back to Trevallyn from the town side. Thereafter I looked for it each time I passed, curious about who lived there, or who had once lived there, for I never saw any sign of life in or around the house. Curtains hung in straight folds at the windows and the sole central chimney never gave off the welcoming smoke that suggested a warm hearth warmed the chill that was almost a permanent part of the Cataract Gorge. I liked the way it perched above the path leading to the cliff grounds, tucked neatly into the cliff face in a juxtaposition of comfort that somehow worked, like the co-dependency of a marriage of opposites. The changing shades of dolerite a water colourist's wash behind the quaintness of the cottage, its Swiss style standing out against the nearby Edwardian and Federation streetscape. Like a scene from a picture book, it beckoned as a story waiting to be stepped into.

With the end of childhood came the beginning of another life, far from the little cottage on the cataract. Other houses caught my attention. Some became mine to live in for a while and joined others that piqued the interest of the emerging writer within. Poems and short stories grew from these imaginings, with other ideas stored away in the conceptual repository of all writers until the time for retrieval was right. There had been times when life events overshadowed the ability to write, when creativity gave way to survival and untidy notes jotted hurriedly in a journal were all I could manage.

It had been a busy and productive life until Levi, a relative by marriage who lived on the knife edge of his delusions, decided to take me with him on his downward fall and I became stuck, caught in a limbo between the mundane safety of normality and the giddy netherworld of his personality disorder. He groomed others, obliterating the memory of previous mutual affection, to rewrite history from his position of transference, ultimately supplanting my positive image with one of his negative preference.

It worked.

His relentless crusade lit the kindling of a post-traumatic stress disorder that paralysed my ability to maintain any reasonable quality of life. I got up each morning as an automaton, thoughts fixated on the coming of night when I could return to bed and escape the misery my waking hours had become. Intention to write each day dissolved into hours spent rifling through posts on social media to find his latest threat, telling myself it was better to know, better to keep my enemies close, unable to comprehend I was re-traumatising myself with each repeat reading. Sometimes weeks passed with no new stalking activity and I'd fool myself I could salvage something of my former life. I'd write a poem, draft a short story, and feel a return of optimism before an abusive hate-filled email slid through my inbox and I'd tumble back into that dark place where death offered the only path to light.

People disappeared from my life as friends and family made excuses to avoid contact with me, citing busy lives, other commitments, pretexts I was too quick to accept, unwilling to admit what was happening. I pretended not to notice a distant flatness in the voices of the disinterested, desperate to hold my family as I'd always known it together, yet one by one they joined the hate club. Hardest to accept was that no one ever told me directly what I had done to become so reviled. Emails offered little insight, citing only, 'things you've done to that poor man'. I assumed this referred to Levi, however, any request for clarification resulted in a further barrage of hate-filled words which, while lacking any factual accusations, broke me almost beyond restoration.

It was hard to comprehend how those I loved, and who had once cared for me in return, now looked on me with contempt, giving me no opportunity to defend myself against the allegations. I had become something less than human in their eyes, a creature to be reviled as evil. As part of his depersonalisation and objectification of me, he stopped referring to me by name, adopting offensive terminology as subliminal coercion of others to distance them from the relationship. He moved from the more benign, *your mother* and *your grandmother*, to deeper, sinister name calling, *the evil one*, *the witch* etc. to desensitise others beyond the normal moral and ethical constraints that govern human interaction.

He defamed my character and diminished my credibility, creating situations where he attributed the abuse inflicted by him to me. In this manner he recruited friends, colleagues, family members and authorities to his cause, provoking collective sanctions of condemnation, contempt and social exclusion.

Now and again there'd be a respite of sorts and I'd know this meant he had someone else in his sights, someone who had offended him in some small way they probably had no awareness of. It was how he rolled, but understanding the classic behaviours of Personality Disorders doesn't necessarily equip a person to deal with them. I knew his vilification was often, as in my case, against people who had stood up against some form of unfairness, abuse, or entitlement quite unrelated to him, but knowing this didn't make it any easier.

His campaign against me was a covert operation that had started months or possibly years before I became aware of it. As a police officer, he bent the law and manipulated it to his advantage to fabricate charges and evidence against those who remained close to me.

When I learnt he was soliciting connections to burn down my home as I slept, I moved several hundred kilometres away and took steps to secure my safety where possible, and then the smear campaign against me ramped up another notch. Using deception and exaggeration to cultivate mistrust, he played on the sensibilities of others and exploiting their empathy to influence them in his favour. Many were passive participants who believed the stories he told, others became actively involved in spreading them further.

Ostracized and isolated, I watched from the sidelines as he played the victim, the hero, and sometimes both at the same time, manipulating others into believing they were good people rightfully standing up against my supposed immorality or abuse.

I tried to address his behaviour through what I believed to be the correct channels, contacting the police ethical standards department as a means of gaining support and appropriate treatment for him. Unfortunately, brotherhood entitlement runs deep beneath the blue calm of the surface and his actions were either covered up or denied completely, other officers backing up his persecution through the courts and adding to his sense of privilege and self-righteousness.

. I lost followers from my social media pages and friends

4

stopped leaving comments on my posts. It hadn't made sense until I was sent a copy of an email sent from an untraceable account. I recognised his use of language in the repetition of words like *wicked, evil, karma,* and hints of an imminent well deserved death. In this group message, he had outlined all of his complaints about me, the wrongs he claimed I had done to him and those who now followed him, and how I brought harm to anyone who had contact with me.

It was a vile missive, full of distortions and lies, yet I could see it would be believable in the persuasive terminology he used. He closed with a request the recipient not reveal the message to me, stating I would bring destruction to them if this happened. Unbelievably naive, yet it worked. I became so fearful I avoided social media for almost a year, always unprepared for the threats of death and karma that was closing in on me and any family members he perceived to be close to me.

Most terror provoking were the middle of the night visits I'd be unaware of until I had a shower the following day, when the water ran cold and I'd realise the gas had been turned off at the meter, or days I'd go outside to find something moved in the yard or a ladder placed against one of the bedroom windows. On other occasions I'd arrive home to find evidence of someone having been inside the house during my absence, a previously locked window left slightly ajar, smoke alarm hanging from the ceiling, or my underwear drawer open and the contents disturbed. I understood the cat and mouse game behind these acts as his way of letting me know he could get me anytime he chose. I became too afraid to sleep in case I didn't hear him coming, getting up numerous times throughout the night to check and recheck all windows and doors were firmly locked. The slightest sound had me creeping about in the dark to peer through the curtains, jumping at shadows and unable to distinguish between the normal sounds of life and those I had come to fear.

Realising the harassment was unlikely to stop and determined to take back control of my life, I began therapy to work through the layers of fear under which he had covered me. It wasn't easy to change patterns of my behaviour and reflexive responses to his guerrilla warfare, but gradually I found a new purpose beyond the fear and heartbreak and began to write once again.

Adopting a pseudonym helped me step aside from the misery that had held me back for so long and strengthened my rebirth into a safer world. I woke each day with a renewed passion to write. I published a couple of books and won a few awards for short stories and poetry, but I wanted something more. I wanted to write the story that had been clawing at my insides since my first sight of the cottage snuggled against the cliff face, all I needed was the opportunity to bring it to reality.

I had lost too many years dancing on the end of Levi's paranoia when the possibility of a life change presented itself in the form of an out of state writer's residency. Three months to spend in almost seclusion apart from obligations to participate in selected community events, a small price to pay for the peace and tranquillity of living in the cottage of my childhood memory and time to write.

In my eagerness to escape the present, I had forgotten the darker history of the river.

Cherubs without wings

Their stories

The river has two faces, one gives life to the city, the other snatches life from the unwanted and unsuspecting, a watery cradle of unrest.

***

I've been here the longest, over one hundred and seventy years, dying the same day I was born, an act of brutal murder that no one was ever brought to justice for.

It was a worker from the marine department who found me. He saw something that looked like a woman's apron in the water in about two feet water, just out from the wharf. He caught it with a boat-hook and the cloth gave way before he managed to get a grip on it to reveal my tiny body tied up in the bloodied handkerchief that had been pinned together. The bundle had been tied up in an apron with a large rock to weigh it down and thrown into the water during the hours of darkness.

I'd been born alive and then battered around the head and face with such force it left a wound on the right side of my face extending from my mouth to below the right ear and inside my mouth. There were other ways to silence my cries and attempts had been made to choke me, but I didn't die quickly enough to suit them so they resorted to other means. My skull was fractured in three places and there were two penetrating wounds on the right side of the head corresponding with the seat of one of the fractures.

My mother and her co-murderers were never found and

without any identifying information the coroner returned a verdict of 'wilful murder against some person or persons unknown'.

If I wasn't wanted and my mother didn't have someone to care for me, she could have left me on a doorstep where someone may have found me. Better to be a foundling than to be dead. Or she could have smothered me easily enough because I couldn't have defended myself could I, newly born as I'd been.

I cry almost every night and some think I'm crying for my mother or from the pain of my injuries, but I don't shed a tear for the one who battered me to death. I cry to be released from this place, to lie in a warm cradle, to be held in loving arms. I know there's a way out of this place. Martha tells me to be patient and I try, I really do, but the years pass slowly.

***

My casket was a piece of winsey cloth and my grave the mud of the North Esk River. If I hadn't been spotted by a man crossing the Tamar Bridge, I would probably have washed further down river with the next high tide. He had noticed an object lying on the mud where the tide has receded and, on closer inspection, saw my tiny foot poking out from the piece of cloth in which I'd been wrapped, which had come undone as the two ends had not been tied. I had been placed in my watery grave a few hours earlier, meeting death from a blow to the head and bleeding out from an untied umbilical cord. The law eventually caught up with my mother, although she denied any wrong doing and no one seemed inclined to tell the truth at her trial, not those who could have shed some light on events anyway. It was as much my grandmother's fault, more really, as it was she who decided my fate, delivering and dispatching me within minutes of my birth.

Life was cheap for many of her ilk who'd come to the colony via convict ships and I wouldn't be the first nor the last to end up in a muddy grave. They found my mother and committed her for trial on the evidence of the cloth I'd been wrapped in. If I could, I'd tell my mother that I understand it wasn't her fault, that she'd been let down by the very people who should have cared for her – for me too.

***

I was in the river four weeks before they found my body near the railway bridge, still attached to a piece of string tied around a large stone wrapped in a cloth. My death had been occasioned by a violent blow to the back of my head.

***

They found my small body in the water off the Esplanade. My hands and legs had been tied together and a string passed round under my naked body. I had no covering, no name, and no one to mourn my passing.

***

I washed up near the rowing sheds, wrapped in a black jacket and covered with brown paper, a surprise and a cruel find for the small boy who found me. Smothered in the hours after my birth I took part of my mother with me with her long hair held tightly in my fist. I was born strong and fought hard to live, but her need to be rid of me was stronger.

***

The tides had a way of carrying many of us onto the mud and discovery. Members of the North Esk Rowing Club, who were out on the river, disturbed the old carpet in which my body had been wrapped. The means of my death, a handkerchief tied tightly around my neck, had been left intact. The water had been the burial place for many of us, tossed aside as so much rubbish for the river to determine our fate. Some, like me, were caught by the tide and laid gently in the mud, while so many others were carried away to nothingness. Neither wanted in life nor acknowledged in death.

***

They say Limbo is a temporary state for those who die without baptism or mortal sin, yet the term is undefined. So, as theologians debate the issue, we await mercy and forgiveness for our killers in this place of unrest. Only this will bring about our release and still the cries of the damned.

Chapter 2

Stepping off the plane onto the tarmac, almost four decades after I'd last said goodbye to the island, it was as if I had never left, as if my life in the intervening years had never existed. And with this, the fear that had weighted the trip to the airport and the interminable wait to board the flight, that Levi would somehow sabotage my plans, disintegrated.

It had been a smooth transition to a new life, one of those Tasmanian days when the wind whipped anything not anchored down and the rain hit the ground so hard it bounced back to meet itself coming down, but I saw only the sun of the days to come.

I'd weighed up the pros and cons of starting out with a new identity, the loss of recognition for earlier achievements and empty spaces on what had once been a complete CV, in exchange for another chance at life. It hadn't been my intention to create a fictitious past as much as remain mysterious, with selective use of facts to avoid suspicion. Francesca Ashbury was now the name on my driver's licence, credit cards and all personal identification. I had opened social media accounts under this identity and developed a large enough following to be found on Google. Clare Towns had been expunged and it was Francesca Ashbury who set out to meet the council officer for my orientation to the residency.

The path to the cottage began at the tollhouse, winding around the edge of the steep cliffs that buttress the gorge before opening out to the landscaped cliff grounds. When the area became a popular picnic in the late 18th century, the town council constructed the tollgate and the caretaker's cottage beyond, built precariously on the side of the cliff. The premise was the husband worked the grounds while his wife collected the toll fees.

It had been a hurried introduction to the cottage. Jana, the council officer responsible for the *Artist in Residence Program*, wavered between welcoming me to the city and attributing any shortfall in her knowledge to the temporary nature of her position. She gave me a rushed tour through the rooms, handed me the folder containing the rules and expectations and waived aside any questions I may have had with an all-encompassing, 'it's all in the folder'.

I played the part of the visitor, eager to show appreciation at being accepted as writer in residence at the iconic cottage, suppressing impatience to begin the writing experience. She left in a flurry of last minute instructions as to the use of the security alarm, shuffling papers into an outsized shoulder bag in preparation for her next appointment.

And then I was on my own. Alone in the silence that minutes before had been masked by conversation of two strangers trying to appear at ease with each other and I was face to face with the fear of an absent muse. Others might think it was premature to worry about such things, but experience had taught me to make an early start, to write something, anything, to blot the face of the blank page. I began to throw words around in my mind, knowing as soon as I had something written down I could relax into the longer task. Like undercoating or priming prior to painting a wall, I hoped this would provide a solid base to build on.

I wandered through the cottage to familiarize myself with its layout, two small living spaces set up as a living room and a study, one bedroom, a bathroom and an economy size kitchen. Quite big enough for my needs, but it revived my curiosity about the families who had lived here during its days as the caretaker's cottage and how they'd fitted within its confines. History hung in layers on the bones of the old building and I wished the walls could talk to connect me with its past.

I transferred these thoughts into words, jotting them down before they flew to that unreachable place of the writer's hiraeth, leaving me to grieve their loss while never quite remembering exactly what it was I had lost, knowing only it may been something special. Words fell into lines and formed a framework for the poem to follow. I scribbled and mused and scribbled some more until, satisfied to have made a start, I set about making the place my own.

I unpacked the few clothes I had brought with me, jeans and jumpers suitable for the colder weather fitted easily into the deep drawers of the dresser, and the one good outfit for less casual outings hung lonely in the wardrobe that dominated the wall facing the bed. I had brought two coats, both so ancient in the world of fashion they were probably due to come back into vogue, hanging these on the coat rack near the front door with scarves for company, similar to their placement at home with my boots on the floor nearby. I never bothered with the sentiment of photos next to the bed or the trapping of emotion in ornaments. I carried my loved ones in my heart to keep them close.

The kitchen took even less time to set up. Coffee, long life milk, a four pack of yoghurt, two minute noodles, wine, crackers and cheese, and I was done. It was a good thing I travelled light with food too, considering the miniscule size of the fridge. The bottles of wine, one red, one white, I left standing on the benchtop next to the empty fruit bowl.

By the time I had put my laptop on the desk in the study, I was at home as I needed to be. The electric heater hummed a warm welcome and it was only as I tried the one armchair for comfort that I noticed darkness had fallen.

With this came silence.

Not the quiet that blocks out all sound, for I could still hear the low hum of traffic as it crossed one or the other of the two bridges that spanned the river. This stillness was more a reminder of my separation from the rest of population.

There was me and the cottage and beyond that the cataract and surrounds, and that was the limit of my night world. Tell myself this was what I had wanted, I settled down with a sachet coffee to read, reflect, and write.

A requirement of the residency had been to create a work relating to the cottage or the Cataract Gorge reserve, as other writers and artists had done since the inception of the program, and I had a rough outline of the story I intended to write. Jana had mentioned reports of past residencies kept in a folder in the study and I rifled through the assortment of books and papers on the shelves until I found a binder, bulging with plastic sleeves and papers of all sizes.

Some artists had supplied photos or other examples of the work they'd undertaken and I was impressed. All were glowing in their praise of the cottage and their experience in general and this affirmed I had made the right decision in coming here. The volume and quality of work created by others increased my impatience to merge with my surroundings and begin my own and I hoped three months would be sufficient time.

Shutting down one sense to magnify others, I closed my eyes, letting the scent of the cottage wash over and around me bringing images of other times and other lives. The age of the wood panelling blended with the dampness of the river but, overpowering this was the aroma of ash from a wood burning fire, of damp clothes and water in a kettle just boiled, evoking memories of earlier times.

Other writers before me had described this place as the playground of their childhood, however, while the cataract had formed a large part of my growing up years, this wasn't how I defined it.

For me, the area had mostly been a place of foreboding, the green waterway unpredictable, and I'd cower close to the railing as I crossed the bridge fearful the river would rise up and snatch me. The stone quarry on the other side, its tattered fringe of aged cypress hinting at the dark secrets of its convict past, sheltered bearded hermits in tattered clothes who lived in and around the cliffs. Somehow, the demons of my imagination had more substance than reality and if I overcame my dread of the river or the quarry, the grinding murmurs coming from inside the old flour mill were the starting gun that set my heart racing. It had always been a relief to reach solid ground and the relative safety of Paterson Street, the leather soles of my shoes slapping victory, until the next crossing.

Even travelling on the bus had potential for danger. Each single lane approach began and ended with a sweeping bend and I had nightmares in which the bus failed to straighten and crashed through the rails to the water below. In my dreams I always free fell in slow motion, waking just before I hit the water. I had been told if you hit the ground, or water, in a falling dream you'd die on impact, a knowledge that did nothing to lessen the terror or the jolt of waking abruptly to the dissolving nightmare. This had been a recurring dream throughout my life, the sensation of falling and the sound of the river rushing toward me. I blamed the river.

Eager to move away from this memory, I switched my recall to further up the gorge to the First Basin and more pleasant memories of warm days spent lying on the freshly mown grass in anticipation of the next dip in the pool. But even sunny day memories could cloud over as quickly as the weather changes that threatened to disrupt even the clearest of summer days, when great thunderheads appeared out of nowhere to begin a dark march across the sky. With the sudden change in weather, the cliff face surrounding the pool area frowned as it closed in on itself and swimmers ran from the pool, grabbing towels and picnic baskets and small children dragging their feet, vacating the area as the vanquished flee before an advancing army.

Only the foolhardy continued swimming and clowning until the first streamers of lightning hit the ground, turning the amphitheatre into a pressure cooker of ozone, and then they too fled, earlier parental warnings of storm survival rumbling in thunder.

Now I was back in this place that had formed the backdrop to my childhood. Not just passing by, but living eating and sleeping for the next three months in the cottage of my curiosity. Despite the decades that had passed, strip away the years and I was the same person beneath the veneer of adulthood and recent name change, and the gorge itself hadn't changed in aeons.

There was now another bridge swooping across on the town side of the old bridge, built in the seventies when aesthetics had been sacrificed for the sake of expedience. Sweeping concrete stanchions dwarfed the cast iron railings of its older partner, shunting it into the background as if it was now less worthy. No different to many people's attitude to older folks or anything considered to be past its use by date, pushed to the back of the shelf and hidden behind newer, flashier products.

The quarry had been filled in years ago with a theme

park motel that fooled most of the tourists into thinking it had been there since European settlement, slipping so well into its surrounds many locals had forgotten it hadn't always been there. But the gorge itself was the same, a few hundred or thousand less cusecs flowing down the rapids, depending on the release rate or the season, since the hydro dam had been built upriver in the fifties, the twin cliff faces remained unchanged.

These had been my thoughts as I penned the outline of the poem. Not letting myself listen to the silence or think beyond the moment, I reached back for the excitement I'd felt when first setting out on this venture, opening the doors to the narrow balcony to stand at the railing, blinking to adjust my vision to the dark lens of night. Beyond the bridges the city lights gave off the yellow glow of civic life after dark, a subdued light that matched a slower pace of life. The town clock chimed across the low profile of rooftops and I tapped my fingers against the wooden balustrade to count the hours, comforted by its solid and reliable presence. It had been my companion of the night as a child when I'd been unable to sleep, listening for safe sounds to take me from the darkness of my bedroom to places of kinder imagination. I was comforted by the reconnection.

Beneath the balcony, the path to the cataract grounds snaked until it disappeared around a deep bend and below this the precipitous rock face led down to the water, its daytime green now a coverlet of nervous silk that moved in aggressive restlessness in the moonlight. Now and again the sharp slap against rocks was interrupted by a flash of silver as an exuberant fish took momentary flight, plopping on re-entry before others joined the game. The river was preparing for the season of deluge and I was surprised the fish hadn't already headed for the sanctuary of calmer waters. I no longer felt alone as I closed the door and went about the business of spending my first night in the cottage.

The bedroom had been decorated country cosy, the smell of the huon pine dresser pungent and clean. The bed creaked, almost a groan, as I sat on the edge where other writers and artists had sat and slept before me. I lay back against the pillows, hoping some of their creative dust remained to fall my way. By the light of the bedside lamp, a squat ceramic with a coolie shade and low watt bulb, I leafed through some of the books I had purchased as reference material. Dry tomes most of them, but I marked pages for further reading with fluoro stickits I had brought for the purpose, before the dimness of sleep misted my vision and the book lay where it fell at the side of the pillow. In the fugue state of half sleep, I heard the sound of wind in the sheoaks, the creaking of old timbers and the far off wail of a child or an animal, before pulling the eiderdown up from the bottom of the bed and covering myself with sleep.

I awoke to birdsong as daylight mottled the opposite side of the gorge. There was a poem in there somewhere and this heartened me as I played around with a few lines while showering, the first syllables of a haiku, something to be going on with and connect me with place. I didn't write a lot of haiku, understanding there was more to the form than simply rattling off three syllable-measured lines, however, I was happy with this one and set it aside to revise and add to over the coming days and weeks until I had a linked suite.

The first day was a free day as far as community obligations attached to the residency. After that there'd be workshops to facilitate and writing events to attend and as much as I looked forward to these, I was grateful for the time to familiarise myself with my new surroundings and reintroduce myself to places once known.

I hadn't had a chance to look around outside when I had arrived the day before and made this my first task after breakfast, taking my coffee out to the paved area at the rear of the cottage with the idea of a leisurely stroll around the yard. I was disappointed to see that, while the sun shone on the town side of the gorge, it didn't extend its warmth to the rear of the cottage and I could see it would rarely do so at this time of the year, if ever. Water drizzled a slow path down the rocks to pool on any flat surface, however small, the run-off dripping onto the moss covered pavers below. The smell of damp earth and foliage filled the air, taking my breath. I decided there'd be no leisurely breakfasts or al fresco writing in this backyard for me.

My exploration was over as quickly as it begun, its postage stamp size able to be taken in at a glance. Rising up behind the cottage a sheer dolerite cliff face dominated, reaching skyward in a jigsaw of massive boulders and determined vegetation that tufted out from crevices to fan the lichen clinging to the rock. It was unlikely anyone would be dropping in from behind or from the west side of the house either, both almost as one with the rocks that supported it. With the frontage elevated above the cliff path, the only entrance was the way I'd come in the day before, up the steep steps cut into the rock, almost hidden if you didn't know to look for them, with entry through a latched gate and across the paved courtyard to the front door.

The traffic on the bridges ramped up as commuters made their way to work, and early morning joggers dashed past for what I was to learn was a regular route for many, taking them up one side of the gorge, through the cataract grounds and over the suspension bridge to the rugged zigzag track leading back to the town side. I hadn't done a lot of walking in recent years, but felt I was up to the challenge if I took it easy. Putting this walk on my to do list for later that day, I settled down in the sitting room with my research books. I had thought of sitting out on the deck but had to acknowledge that with so many diversions, I'd get little reading done and I wanted to make a start on the gathering of the facts and figures that would add authenticity to my novel. It was also icy cold, wind sneaking in through invisible gaps between windows and walls to lift the edges of papers I had placed on the desk, whistling the lyrics of the storm to come. All I needed was a fire blazing in the grate to complete the picture of comfort of my imagination, but the chimney had been removed years before and I had to content myself with the impersonal but efficient electric heater.

By mid-morning I had several pages of notes typed out, and new plot lines chasing each other inside my head that needed clearing before I wrote anything further. I packed a backpack with bottled water, notebook and camera, eschewing the heavier DSLR for the more compact point and shoot, and set out. I could have used the camera on my phone for convenience, but I preferred the more intimate involvement with images that came through the camera lens and I never knew when I'd need a higher resolution image. Old fashioned, I guess, or just old, getting closer to that dreaded use by date.

I do a lot of writing in my head, particularly during the planning stages or when the story threatens to become bogged down. It's something I can do anywhere at almost any time; sitting in the car, hanging out the wash, house cleaning, waiting for appointments, times when I let my mind go into serendipitous free fall and picked out what I needed later. I knew today this could work on many fronts as I soaked up the atmosphere of what was to be the broader setting for the story, taking in the sights, sounds, smells and sensations of the area.

The river had risen overnight to form an impressive cascade. Not quite the roar I remembered, but a determined splashing and dancing of brown foam-flecked water over submerged rocks, the occasional log carried from upstream spearing into the air before deep diving beyond the main fall. Majestic tree ferns, or man ferns as they were called in this state, threw misted fronds skyward as if to catch every errant drop of water, scenting the air with clean dampness.

The walk took much longer than on the stronger, athletic legs of my younger years, so I didn't complete the circuit via the zig zag path, realising my plan had been too ambitious. I stopped at intervals to take a photo or jot down thoughts and observations and had a leisurely coffee at the tearooms. By the time I returned to the cottage, I had six pages of notes and sketches and several dozen images to upload. The buzz from the caffeine was on the wane and it was time to refuel and hunker down for a few hours of transcribing notes and research into a more organised and legible form on the laptop.

Another idea I'd had while on the think trail had been to write daily blog posts about the residency and my activities, keeping these brief and including the drafts of poems and I made this my first task on my return. The blog had only been in place for a couple of years, beginning when the idea of changing identity first took form. It gave an early legitimacy to Francesca Ashbury, writer and poet.

The first night and day of my residency had passed I was filling my new skin with ease.

Eliza

I came in from Lebrina to receive treatment at the General Hospital in Charles Street, staying at a boarding house just over the road. I'd been unwell for some time, ever since I found the lump and knew it was the same condition my mother had suffered before her long and painful death. When the doctors told me there was no cure for me I knew what I had to do.

Dressed in my favourite outfit of dark green skirt and blouse, topped with a straw hat in light grey and matching gloves, I set out for the cataract. The day was fair, not too hot for that time of the year and I enjoyed the walk. In fact the day was so ordinary I could almost convince myself all was fine in my world as I sat by the river and watched water rollicking over and between the rocks. But it wasn't all right and it never would be. I thought about life back in Lebrina with my poor widowed father, both of us missing mother and pretending otherwise to make the most of it. After mother left it went without saying that I'd take on her role. There'd be no marriage for me. No babies or home of my own.

The decision to enter the water was an easy one. I couldn't swim and I knew once I'd stepped off the rock ledge there'd be no turning back. I took off my hat and placed it nearby with my gloves before beginning that last few steps away from life. I didn't want it floating on the surface of the water and perhaps alerting a Good Samaritan who would feel obliged to save me. I didn't know how long it took to drown, whether it was seconds or minutes or even longer. It was a new experience for me. The gloves I removed out of habit, something I always did on removing my hat. These were found not long after by two ladies who handed them into the tollkeeper. They needn't have troubled themselves as I had no further use of them.

I'm glad I never lived to feel the full pain of my illness, but to be confined with this rabble of unhappiness wasn't something I'd planned on either. Sometimes I wonder if this is a room in hell, a place of torture by water where heat from the flames never reaches.

Chapter 3

I was to discover that night came early to the Cataract. The last rays of the setting sun teasing the lichen beard of the rock, winking through the tallest trees before a sudden shutting out of the light. I enjoyed this time the most, the slow winding down of the city at the end of a working day, when traffic on the bridges thinned to a slow hum. It became part of my own ritual, creature habits creeping in to incorporate meals, activities, writing and sleep, although this was becoming more difficult to achieve.

The crying I had heard on the first night that I had attributed to an animal, unable to believe a child would be out at that late hour, had continued on subsequent nights. It had begun as a short wail, progressing on ensuing nights to intermittent calls and shrieking. This was accompanied by soft shuffling inside the cottage, the muted banging in the kitchen on the other side of the bedroom wall and thin whispers of conversation. At first I had been frightened, scared out of my wits to be truthful, and sleep only came in snatches when exhaustion overtook fear for brief periods.

The Levi years were never far from my thoughts when anything out of the ordinary occurred and I had to be constantly on my guard against paranoia. Then I became tired enough, angry enough, to seek out a common sense explanation for the sounds; a bough against the tin roof or the swish of a curtain caught in a draft, both ruled out the following day when I saw there were no trees close enough to the house to touch the roof and no curtained windows, but the possibilities had given me the assurance I needed to get through the hours of darkness.

One night, determined to find the cause of the disturbances, I got down on my hands and knees and crawled about the floor looking for loose carpet, or a mat that might dust the floor with sound when a low breeze crept under the door. This was also crossed of my list of possibilities when I discovered the only room with floor coverings was the bathroom where the vinyl had been glued to the floor boards.

I asked about the cottage, in a casual hinting manner at the groups I attended, trying to glean anecdotal information that could not be found in books, but there wasn't anything I hadn't heard before. There were the odd theories of hauntings by drowning or suicide victims, accompanied by urban myth that had been stretched over the years to tissue thinness and with no substantive evidence. I was on my own with it.

Whether from subconscious choice or sheer fatigue, I developed a pattern of falling asleep in the hours before daybreak and sleeping into the morning, catnapping at times throughout the day as my schedule allowed. This reduced the bags under my eyes to a less conspicuous size and toned down the wild eyed look of the sleep deprived. I even gave some thought to going to a motel for a night or two for an uninterrupted sleep. Determination not to be driven out and a limited budget put an end to that fantasy and I decided if I couldn't beat them I may as well join them. The next time I heard the sound of voices coming from the kitchen I asked them to speak up.

'I appreciate you probably don't want to wake me, but I'm a light sleeper anyway,' a little bit of night craziness added more confidence to my voice than I felt, 'do you mind if I join you?'

I had to ask several times over a number of nights before

I received any discernible answer and then only after I had asked her, and I assumed it was a woman, for her name. But long before I received any reply the sounds from the kitchen became progressively louder, as if the person making the noise wanted to be heard.

'My name's Francesca, and you are...?

The banging stopped and then, after a long pause, a voice answered, 'Martha, I am. Martha Boyd.'

It was at this point I almost gave the whole residency away. It had been one thing to try and make contact, a game really, as I had never really expected an answer.

Or had I?

Lack of sleep had left me prone to delusion and, in my more rational moments, I wondered if Levi had caught up with me and found a new and novel method of torment. Now it was my turn for silence. Suddenly my bed felt cold against my clammy skin, my heart thumping drunkenly as the situation moved from surreal to very real.

'Well, are you still there?'

Berating myself now for ever starting this, I tried to speak with self-assurance, but all I could manage was a thin stutter, 'Yes, yes I'm still here.'

'Well you said you'd like to meet me so best you get yourself out here and let me see you.'

I scuttled sideways out of bed, shoved my feet into the slippers I'd kicked off earlier and shuffled my arms into the sleeves of my old dressing gown, before making my way to the kitchen, turning on every light as I went. If this was a trick I didn't want to be caught in the dark.

An out of character, reckless determination drove my action, or maybe it was borne more from lack of sleep and impulse control. On the other hand, it was only a dream and an exploration of the sub-conscious could provide a rational explanation for the intrusion into my sleep. I just had to remember this and all would be well.

The heat from the kitchen reached into the first sitting room and I could see the glow of a fire as I drew closer, the figure of a woman bending over the hob, her long dress sweeping the floor with each movement she made. Where the walls of the kitchen had been was now a dark mist that moved with other forms, faceless and shapeless in the gloom, all seeming to speak at once in low tones. Strangely though, I had no sense of fear now, and I moved closer in out of body curiosity.

'What are you doing here?' We both asked the question at the same time and a stare off ensued as we sized each other up.

Martha was short in statue, probably not 150 centimetres, or five feet in the old measurement, and as round as she was tall. She drew herself to full height, bosom raised as an Amazon's shield, and asked the question again.

'Well? What are you doing in my cottage? Fancy robbing me, do you?' Titters and open laughs came from around the edge of the gathering, as if she'd said something hilarious. 'Do you think I make enough from the tolls to start giving it away, do you?' She emphasised the end of the question with a jab of the poker in my direction and I stepped back out of reach.

'No, not at all. I think there's been a misunderstanding, for it's me who should be asking who you are.' I began to tell her who I was and the purpose of my visit, but she turned her back on me and began speaking in those irritating whispers with the other women as if I wasn't there.

'Don't trust her,' they said, in one form or another, red capped tricoteuses inciting their leader, 'don't trust her.'

'Keep quiet, Mary Ann,' Martha singled out one voice from the mob, 'I'll deal with this.'

Occasionally the wail of a child calling its mother, or a distant scream, broke the pattern of their murmurs, followed by a hushing or a sharp rebuke, yet I saw no one other than Martha and there was no further acknowledgment of my presence.

Then I was back in my bed with daylight edging through the sides of the blinds and the familiar sound of traffic on the bridge and the patter of passing joggers to bring my world back into balance. Throwing back the covers, I rushed through the house to the kitchen, needing to see it in its usual state, to refute the experience of the previous night.

It was as it should be. The walls were in place. There was no solid fuel stove, no woman in a flowing dress, wailing children or whispered conversations. It had been a vivid dream and one I hoped wouldn't be repeated in a hurry. Such was the curse of the writer's mind, it never knew when to turn off. And yet, even as I poured water from the kettle into my cup I detected, not the rich coffee odour of my anticipation, but the faintest whiff of cold ash I had smelt on my first night in the cottage.

I slept soundly the next few nights, taking more ownership of the residency and my surroundings, eating breakfast on the small balcony rugged up in my old duffle coat to ward off the wind that blew hard off the river. Other times, when the mist added a layer of dampness wherever it touched, I'd slip on my equally ancient rubberised hooded mac, cupping the coffee mug to warm my hands. When weather permitted I walked around the cataract, before settling down to a few hours uninterrupted work and I had a number of poems and Haiku written and several thousand words of my novel, pleased with the progress I'd made.

The interlude with Martha seemed absurd now it was behind me, so much so that I used it as a creative writing exercise in my next workshop. Held at the cottage, I set the atmosphere with a tour of the rooms and an animated description, if somewhat embellished, of the dream. Later, some of the participants thought it amusing to re-enact the scene in the kitchen, barely big enough for one person at the best of time. Apart from the squashing of bodies against the walls and corners of the room, there was an eerie likeness to the whispering giggles that left me feeling uneasy and I was pleased when all returned to the present and sat down to the business of creative writing.

The next part of the session began with the draft of a poem I had posted on my blog. I invited comment on this and other recent work, making notes for later reference before winding down the day. It had been an easy activity for me, as all in attendance wanted to make the most of their time in the cottage and have something to show at the end of it. On a high, I accepted an invitation to dinner at the home of one of the women, Anna, who lived nearby. I had exchanged greetings with her as she jogged past the cottage each morning and I felt as if I already knew her when she had turned up with the group for the workshop.

Peace had returned to my days and nights and I was feeling good.

Very good.

Mary Ann

I was only seventeen when I went into the water. Too young to know what I was doing. Too young to find a way out of the problems of my life. Even as I walked down to the cataract that day I didn't really understand the permanency of my actions, stopping to speak with a couple of young lads in passing. I ran up to them and asked them what they were doing there and I was sorry to see that my manner had frightened them, but I wasn't in my right mind and told them they'd be fishing for me after I jumped off the rock.

Such a stupid thing to say.

The water was cold after the summer heat of the day yet it burnt as it passed through my airways, before I ceded to a sense of peace, a tranquillity I'd never been able to find in life. And then I was floating above the river, watching the activity below as the miller recovered my body and attempted to bring me back to life, but I wasn't coming back. Not ever.

A lot was said after I'd died and those who professed to know me spoke at my inquest with great authority, yet they spoke rubbish, for only I knew why I chose to end my life.

My mother had died before my tenth birthday and my father followed her to the grave six years later although I had been in service long before he went, scrubbing out an existence in the homes of other people. Even before this, our family had struggled. Father had been a convict, sent out from the old country to serve ten years building this society for the benefit of those who would be his betters, working himself into an early grave as Mother had before him. And she had only known hardship herself as the child of two convicts in a fledgling colony.

I'd been trying to make my way in the world, working for the sadler and more recently for the auctioneer, but it was secure room and board I most desperately needed. I was heartily sick of moving from place to place, relying on the goodwill of others. I told my friend, Lizzy, I was going to make away with myself, but just because we'd been laughing at the time she thought I'd been only larking. This is so often the way with sadness that so many hide behind a smile that's only skin deep. Lizzy said I had stayed at her mother's house on Saturday and Sunday nights, but that wasn't true. I'd paid a shilling to stop at the Elephant and Castle on the Saturday and went to Lizzy's place the following night. I'd known her mother for many years and often turned to her in time of need, sharing a bed with Lizzy. The next day I left to go to Mrs Harris's as I never liked to overstay my welcome anywhere, but she hadn't wanted me to stay at her house either, telling me to go to Mr Goode's house. I told her I'd argued with my sister who also wanted me to return to Mr Goode's and I couldn't do as she suggested. Mrs Harris allowed me to stay for one night, advising me to get a place of my own as soon as possible.

Lizzy told the inquest that I was sometimes sulky and ill-tempered for short periods and therefore she didn't take any notice when I'd told her I intended to go and drown myself. She had watched as I crossed the Brickfields towards the Cataract without calling me back or trying to persuade me not to go in the river and that sort of helped make my mind up. I know I never told her why I was going to do this. How could I when I didn't understand it myself, beyond being deeply sad and overcome at times by a sense of hopelessness. I couldn't seem to get lasting employment, working a week here and a week there, leading to a vicious cycle of never enough money and no permanent place to stay.

I was a week working for the sadler and then a week at the auction house, and not sure how long this would last either as it didn't suit me.

I went to see my sister on the Saturday to pick up some handkerchiefs and a hat I'd left at Mr Goode's house. When she asked why I couldn't go myself I told her I didn't want to go there anymore because he was on to me about keeping bad company. I know he'd been a kind friend to us both since the death of my mother, but I felt I needed to make decisions of my own. I told my sister it was no business of hers where I was staying and I spoke rather sharply, because she also advised me against keeping the company of Lizzy. My father had lived there with his new wife before he died and as she still lived there I considered it a fit place for me stay. It had been good enough for him so why not me?

I left my few belongings at a house in Balfour Street, asking them to keep them until I could get a place. If I'd been able to get a position that suited and a permanent place to live, things may have turned out differently. Even if Lizzy had taken me seriously or someone had offered hope for the future, but there was none and it was this, not a fit of temporary insanity as found by the coroner that took me to the river. I just wanted to meet once again with Mother and Father.

Now all I want is to move from this place where I've waited all these years, a crowded purgatory where there is no going forward or back. Martha speaks of release for us all and to pray that this Francesca woman will be the one to make it happen.

We'll see.

Chapter 4

Later I was to ask myself how opportune the invitation to dinner had really been. It had felt more like an ambush where I had been sacrificed for the entertainment of others. First the introductions to her other guests, followed by the inquisition as to my writer's pedigree, beginning with the usual.

'What have you written before?' This was asked in a voice laden with arrogance, the interest being more in what I hadn't written.

It was one of things I most disliked about being as a writer, the need for certain personalities to erode my value through thinly disguised insults given from a perception of literary supremacy. I had grown used to it over time, developing responses to suit the occasion, but it still irked. I turned away from the worst offender, leaving her to regale the person seated on her left about her own writing, as yet unpublished because she couldn't decide on a publisher. Oh, if it only was that easy, I thought. I've met these people everywhere; they are the voice of authority in any group of writers, the ones who have been writing a novel for almost a decade, while systematically talking down the works of others. They are the grammar police, who use the outmoded rules of their long ago schooling to smother creativity in others and I made every effort to avoid their company.

Conversation turned to the cottage and how I was finding the experience. I kept my replies general, not wanting to set myself up for ridicule and it seemed Anna hadn't enlightened the other guests as to the afternoon's exercise in creative writing, for which I offered up a silent thanks.

'So, how are you finding life in the cottage?'

'Fine, I'm enjoying it very much.'

'It must be exciting for you.'

'It's interesting, that's for sure.'

I'd realised early in the residency that the people of Launceston carried a fascination with the cottage, bringing with it all sorts of mystical and arcane fantasies.

'I'd be too scared to stay there on my own. Aren't you afraid?'

'It took a while to get used to it. You know how it is in a strange bed and the night noises are different to those I'm used to.'

'I always thought it was haunted.'

'Really?' Others had caught up with the conversation and turned their attention to the subject.

'I was told that when I was a child.'

'Probably by your mother to keep you off those dangerous steps,' there was general laughter at this and the woman continued,.

'It was my husband actually. His great great grandfather or something had been one of the first caretakers with his wife looking after the toll gate, Peter and Martha Boyd if I remember right.'

Martha Boyd?

How could I have possibly known that name?

Perhaps I had seen it written somewhere, or read it in my research material and it had lodged in my subconscious.

People responded by trying to extract more information about the Boyds, but the speaker had little else to add and conversation turned from the cottage to family history, where all seemed to have something to add by way of convict ancestry or an impressive lineage from the landed gentry. I nodded and answered when asked specific questions, but my mind was stuck on Martha Boyd.

More red wine followed and I relaxed into the evening, enjoying the company once the topic of conversation moved from writing and the cottage. It was late when I left and by the time I got out of the taxi at the toll gate, I had forgotten all about Martha Boyd and anything else except the need to crawl into bed and sleep. And sleep I did, until late night carousers woke me in their stagger home in noisy revel across the bridge and I was back to fitful dosing, falling back into a deep sleep not long after I'd heard the town clock strike two.

I woke next to pressure at the foot of the bed, like the nudging of a cat changing position, and I moved my ankle in reflex action. The pressure eased and I heard the soft drag of footsteps toward the door. The terror of old fears re-emerged, a reminder of other night noises when Levi had tapped against windows to let me know he was around. I had to remind myself he didn't know of this place and had no way of knowing Francesca Ashbury, but the anxiety remained and the source of the interruption to my sleep niggled.

The scuffing sounds across the floor reminded me the night noises of my childhood and how I had been convinced it was a haunting of ghosts, staying awake for hours each night from fear of what might happen if I fell asleep, paralysed by terror that kept me chained to my bed. These night noses were eventually unmasked to reveal the culprits as fat mud rats seeking refuge from the swollen river in the comfort of my attic bedroom, a memory that brought little comfort to my current situation perched as it was so close to the river.

The raging thirst of an early onset hangover sent me reaching for the bottle of water next to the bed. I patted the bedside table, knocking the lamp off balance as my hand fluttered in search, but where the familiar shape should have been was a murky nothingness. I tried to rationalise its absence by recalling I'd gone straight to bed after arriving home the night before and had simply forgotten to bring it into the room. This was a technique Marcus had taught me during our many therapy sessions, to take long even breaths and look for the obvious, before jumping in the deep end of panic. It usually worked, yet the leadenness of terror refused to budge this time.

I tried to ignore the dryness in my throat, fighting the images of cool running taps and ice clinking against the sides of frosted glass, pulling the doona up higher to blot out the physical world.

I didn't want to get up.

Not yet.

I had almost fooled myself into forgetting about the thirst when a scream and the sound of splashing brought me to full wakefulness.

Damn!

More tomfoolery on the bridge.

Now I was fully awake, I decided to get a drink after all, detouring to look out the window to see what all the noise was about. Lifting the blind, the moon flicked off the river, which had risen since earlier in the day and increased its pace down the narrow gorge, spraying the edge of the balcony in passing.

The kitchen was cold as it always was with a chill that never left the northern side of the gorge, seeping through the floor boards and where the window didn't quite meet the frame to become part of the structure of the building. I filled the glass straight from the tap and on my first attempt to drink something nudged my arm, causing me to miss my mouth and hit the rim of the tumbler against my cheek, spilling a small amount down my front. Raising the glass again there was another thump, delivered with such force most of the contents spilt onto the floor.

'What!' I spun around to face emptiness and that morphing of the walls I'd previously experienced, although there were no shadowy figures this time, just a malevolent hissing that I struggled to decipher.

'Think it's funny to laugh at other people do you?' I recognised Martha's voice and the anger that edged it, 'and here I'd been ready to make friends with you, a stranger in my own home. I knew another Frances once and she was a smart mouth like you. Fell into the river she did, just as I was going down to the tolls. She was lucky though, a passing constable saw her and threw her a rope. She got charged with attempting suicide and she never crossed me again. Be careful, you may not be so lucky.'

'You've got it wrong, Martha. I've never...'

'And I can't stand a liar either. I heard you laughing with your friends. We all heard you.' At this there rose an assenting murmur from where the walls should have been.

I was tired, I was thirsty, my nerves were ragged and I'd had enough of these multi-dimensional nightmares.

'I don't really care what you think. As a matter of fact I don't even believe in you. You're not real. Get it. You're not real so shove that up your clacker because I'm going back to bed.'

I didn't usually speak in this manner, but it was the best response I could come up with in such ridiculous circumstances. I heard a collective inward breath of shock as my words found their mark, throwing a parting shot over my shoulder in passing,

'And my name's Francesca not Frances.'

I almost slipped on the wet floor as I turned and stormed back through the house, a small glimmer of sanity pushing through my anger to ask why, if I didn't believe in Martha, I was so irate.

I was now wide awake, my top wet and cold from where I'd spilt my drink. I was still thirsty and sleep was no longer an option. I threw my old robe on and went out to the study, switching on every light as I went. Like holding a cross out to a vampire, I thought light to be the nemesis of my nocturnal companions and I'd be able to read or even write if the inspiration came, in peace.

I didn't look at the clock and kept my eyes from glancing at the tool bar at the bottom of the screen when I turned the laptop on, a knowledge of time often being the quash of intention. I wanted to see if Martha's name had been mentioned in any of the books I had bought or borrowed for research into the area. I'd been fortunate in finding a publication specific to the Launceston Cataract Gorge that covered everything from flora and fauna to the Caretaker's cottage and I went straight to this chapter. I had to have read the name somewhere for it to be a part of my dreams.

Outside the wind had sprung up and I could hear its mournful cry through the trees high on the opposite cliff top, sounding human-like in the hours of darkness. Now and again it faded to nothing until, just as I had become used to the stillness, a high pitched wail reached through the window and set my heart on that irregular beat of sudden fear. It was the sound of a child crying for its mother, 'Mama, Mama, please...' but I understood how the wind could play tricks on mind in need of sleep and experiencing the thickening of a hangover and did my best to ignore it.

I resisted the temptation to look out the window, feeling this would play to my fear and turned again to the book, tracing my fingers along each line.

Aha! I found it. Martha Boyd!

There she was, mentioned as one of the first women of the cottage. Only a line or two, but it was a relief to see her name, to know I must have seen it before and it had embedded itself in my subconscious. I opened a new file on the computer and named it *Women of the Cataract*, typing in the names of all the women mentioned in the book as well as the years they had been at the cottage, before setting this aside for later use. The concept of the women and children who had once shared this space interested me and I wanted to find out more about them. Quite aside from the dreams, which had now taken a step back from the emergent information, I could see the Cataract Gorge offered a much bigger story than the contemporary environment I had intended to use as the setting for my novel.

I opened another document and titled it, *Frances*, for this was another thing I wanted to follow up on and then I went online to *Trove*, the digitised newspaper site for Australian newspapers, and typed *Frances gorge suicide* into the search bar. A few adjustments later and I had an item from around the time Martha and her husband had lived in the cottage. This was a bit creepy. I knew I hadn't read about this before and thought it strange how it had come to me in a dream. I read about the attempted suicide by eighteen year old Frances O'Byrne who had thrown herself into the river and been rescued by a police constable. She had been seen crossing the rocks towards the water's edge by the Martha Boyd, who thought her behaviour suspicious and called out to ask if she was all right. Frances had called back at her to mind her own business and continued on her way and the matter was reported to the police. The constable arrived at the scene just as Frances jumped into the water. A rope had been thrown to her, and she caught it and was saved. She'd told the police that she was tired of her life. Her mother was dead and her employer, with whom she'd been living, had treated her so cruelly she was driven to the rash deed she'd attempted. One week later, she was charged with having attempted suicide by drowning and bound over to be of good behaviour for six months.

That was harsh. First of all the girl had been so depressed she decided she no longer wanted to live and then she had been not only publicly shamed through the newspaper, but also charged with this as an offence.

Poor namesake Frances.

I wondered what Martha had to do with this or whether her comment had been nothing more than a spiteful boast on her part.

Frances

If a person, after careful consideration, determines to take their own life then it is of no business to any other person. Finding myself in the family way and unable to name the father for fear of repercussions, for he had no business lying with me and I had no say in the matter, I saw no way out of my troubles other than death. That old biddy from the cottage stuck her nose in and next thing I knew the police were there and I grabbed the rope they threw to me from pure instinct. Then I got charged with the crime of attempted suicide and the whole town knew about it. I had no choice after that other than to hide my condition and to give birth on my own when my time came.

It had been a girl, but there'd been no time for sentiment. I saw no good purpose in bringing a child into a world that was so cruel and unforgiving and I could not afford to be discovered, so I placed a pillow over her face until she was still. She had fought against death, as hard I had fought against life, snatching my hair and letting go only as the breath left her body. Then I wrapped her tightly in my old chemise and went for a walk by the river, the package carried under my shawl. Luck had been with me as no person saw me out and about at that hour of the night and I was back at my duties at daybreak the next day.

The baby eventually became one of Martha's brood of river foundlings, but she never knew I was the mother, not even after I found myself at the cottage after my death the following year. I had found a sturdy tree away from prying eyes and took a leap of faith into what I'd hoped would be a better place. It wasn't, and I've been here ever since. They say deliverance is coming soon and there's a crowd of us waiting to board the carriage.

Chapter 5

The whole notion of gorge-associated deaths interested me. I hadn't been the only one to see the place as having a presence that invited some to their deaths. I delved further into the archives to find another suicide the following year, successful this time and I empathised with Martha in having these events play out on her doorstep where she couldn't avoid them even if she had wanted to. Then there would have been the sightseers, those who follow tragedy by chasing fire trucks or tracking down the wail of an ambulance, the rubberneckers who gain morbid satisfaction through viewing the tragedy of others. Martha would have had difficulty avoiding these as they'd all have to pass through the toll gate to reach the death sites. Still, I didn't have much sympathy to waste on Martha when she'd had little enough to spare for Frances, even if this had only been in my dream.

I understood not all suicides came from depression or altruism, as I had once thought, but may come about simply because one is tired of living or from a broken heart hidden behind a façade of affability. Reading about another, well-planned and orchestrated suicide I wondered what Martha, as pragmatic as she appeared to be, might have made of this event and the gossip it would have brought to her doorstep, or if she'd had time to think about it before the next one just a month later, when another woman eschewed a watery grave in favour of a seventy foot dive from the top of the quarry onto the rocks below. Thinking back to the feelings aroused by this place during my childhood, I could see how each death had left its mark and added to the dark invitation it offered to a person in a state of despair.

I dozed off in the chair and when I woke, the black of night had ceded to the gloom of morning, a low lying mist limiting vision to arm's length, with no sense of what lay beyond. It reminded me of the chance I had taken when I stepped through the mist as Clare Towns and emerged the other side as Francesca Ashbury, a chance for a new beginning, but no place for the depressed.

Weary of maudlin thought and feeling suddenly hungry, I set books and laptop aside to begin the day. The screams of the wind and the childlike wails it carried had settled down to spasmodic gusts, not strong enough to deter early morning joggers, but loud enough to mask the burr of nearby traffic. The mist parted long enough for the brooding grey of the sky to show beyond the rocks, before closing in again and wrapping the cottage against the world. The smattering of rain on the roof suggested this would be a good day to stay indoors. My research had given me a few ideas to work on and I jotted these down while they were still fresh in my mind before wandering toward the kitchen to make breakfast. I had been so engrossed in research I hadn't even thought about coffee. Now it was what I most wanted and I headed straight for the kettle as I stepped down the small step from living room and then, whoosh!

I skidded across the short space between doorway and wall, hitting the floor with my knee and spinning sideways as I gathered momentum before my head cracked against the wall and the world faded in a giddy spin.

When I regained consciousness I could see through the window to where a weak sun was doing its best to cheer the rock face, but I was wet and it was freezing in this room where the sun never quite reached. When I'd come out to the kitchen to make breakfast, I had forgotten about the water spilt during the night, but that had only been a splash, nothing like the river I'd slid into. Even after my terry cloth robe had absorbed a lot of it, I could see the floor was still sodden, with three puddled areas now connected by my slide.

Terrific, there must have been a roof leak.

My head hurt and so did any part of my body I tried to move and my knee had swollen and taken on the mottled hue of an early bruise. I was hurt, hungry, thirsty and feeling sorry for myself. The residency had started out full of promise and quickly disintegrated into a series of dreams that imitated life and vice versa. But no matter if I was half dead, I was going to have a coffee even if it killed me in the effort. With this goal in mind I crawled and dragged my way across the floor to where I could pull myself up on the door frame. From there it was a short slow slide to the kettle and my world would right itself once again.

If only.

Catherine

I'm not like some of these cry-babies here. I never cry. I learnt that long before I was lost to the river. I always knew my mother didn't want me. I got in the way of her lifestyle as a prostitute in the Old Cross Keys Hotel brothel. I suppose it's a miracle in a way that I managed to live as long as I did, although this was due mainly to the woman into whose care my mother had placed me. When she had left town to work in the Ringarooma tin mines, she handed me back.

Mother was a bit the worse for wear after a day on the drink, staggering as she dragged me with her on the walk to the river. I was afraid. I was always afraid around her, never knowing what she might do next. One minute she'd put me on her knee and coo over me, the next she'd be dragging me across the floor to be tossed aside as a piece of garbage. Just as she'd thrown me in the river, holding me down in the icy water as I begged her, between gasps, to let me go. I was still promising to be a good girl and stay out of her way when the reeds caught in my throat and the bubbles of my last breath drew me down into the darkness where I've been ever since.

She hadn't been a kind mother. She had been very cruel and used to beat me, even when others checked her for this. The kindest thing she'd ever done for me had been to place me in the care of another. She often said she'd do away with me, but people thought this was just the drink and temper speaking. And some continued to believe this, even when evidence showed otherwise, with my mother lying about my whereabouts when questioned by the police after my body had been found.

She was placed at the bar, charged with my murder and found guilty, with a strong recommendation to mercy when she was sentenced to death. The Executive later granted a reprieve, commuting her sentence to imprisonment for life. In the end she served only ten years and later married and had children to whom she was a loving mother.

All these years I have wondered what it was about me that made me so unlovable, like so many of the other babies who gather at the cottage. I want to know why she killed me, for the knowing of this will set me free.

Chapter 6

The accident turned out to my advantage, keeping me cottage-bound for the next couple of days and giving me uninterrupted research time. It was a strange thing about the cottage. During the day it was benign, a place of peace and calm, even when the weather was bitter outside. It was as if, like the twin aspects of the gorge itself, it had two faces of its own. One to show the world, the smiling daytime vista of the quaint cottage, the other a darker side reserved for its occupants during the night.

The rain that had begun before dawn had returned with intensity and maintained a steady beat as the day progressed and I wasn't surprised to see the ceiling was sound, with no sign of leakage in the kitchen or anywhere else. There was no logic to anything connected with this place.

I must have spilt more water than I had realized in my half sleep state. Liquid was like that. You only had to look at red wine spilt on a white cloth. Spill just one drop and it looked like a bucket full. The polished floorboards in the kitchen wouldn't have helped either, with no absorption and the cold night, it would have just lain there, waiting for the unsuspecting. Strange how it had landed in three separate spots though. I supposed it had simply leapt in different directions as it left the glass.

Once, long ago, I'd stepped down onto a log hidden by long grass while holding a cup of coffee and lost my balance as the log began to roll. On my slow descent to the ground, I watched the liquid leave the mug and sail through the air toward my son standing nearby. The next sight, made from a prone position on the ground where I had landed, was of my son blinking through coffee'd lashes, dreadlocks dripping in confusion.

So little liquid, so much wetness.

I packed these thoughts away and settled down to a morning's work, moving between books, genealogy web sites and digitised newspapers. I placed the coffee table so it ran the length of the right side of my chair, providing more space for the pile of books, papers, food and drinks. This is how I had envisaged the residency to be; the cliché of the writer of my imagination.

I wasn't sure why I had begun researching people more than place. Whether from curiosity or instinct, I was prepared to let it lead me for the moment, noting ideas that had potential as poems or short stories. This early into the residency, with a few poems already in first draft and the bones of the novel assembled, I could afford to explore other avenues.

Continuing on from where I had left off earlier, tracking other deaths in the area and matching these with the caretakers at the time, I realised several tragedies had occurred under Martha's watch, with the next one a year later when a young married woman had been found drowned in the First Basin on a Friday evening.

A young boy had been fishing at the gorge, crossing to the centre island where he fished for four or five hours. On his return that evening he saw a body, face downwards in the water, about three or four metres from the bank. Getting help from a man at the picnic grounds and some sailors from a man-of-war, they got the body out. The boy had been fishing the other side and heard no scream or splash, and it was only on returning that he saw the body in the water. Artificial respiration, a forerunner to CPR, was used but it was too late to save the woman. Not a suicide this time. It transpired that the victim had low blood pressure, suffered from fainting fits if she stooped and lately had haemorrhaged from the lungs. Those who knew her didn't think she would attempt to take her life as she had made arrangements to join her husband in Western Australia. A basket, umbrella, and a book were found close to the bank of the river, and on the top of the basket an envelope with deceased's name and address. An inquest returned a verdict of death by drowning, but there was no evidence as to how she got into the water.

The reference to men-of-warships in the Tamar River intrigued me. The term was an old expression first applied to armed naval vessels in the British Royal Navy. Later, it also referred to other large warships such as Frigates, Corvettes, and Brigs. The thought of ships of this size coming into Launceston would be unimaginable today, as the channel had long silted up and the rotting pylons of the old wharves hadn't played host to ships for many years. It had once been a thriving port, even during my own childhood, but it was now not much more than a river of mud with a layer of water over it at high tide, a soft landing for anyone contemplating jumping from either bridge.

But this was another tragic death and the subsequent activity that followed would again have been almost impossible for Martha to avoid. Her husband, as caretaker for all the cliff grounds, would also have come into contact with the activity and any person with an interest in the event. It would have been only natural for both to discuss these happenings at the end of the day, bringing the misfortunes of others inside the walls of the cottage. I made a few notes and continued, wanting to complete my file on Martha by end of day. I understood the family had stayed at the cottage until about 1906 so I didn't have far to go.

The next death recorded was a young boy who had fallen from the rocks. He had gone up the gorge with two mates on a fishing expedition and selected a spot for himself while his companions went further along the gorge. The place he had chosen was dangerous, not far from the cottage where the rocks were steep and slippery. Although his cries attracted the attention of several people close by, they were unable to swim and, with no boat handy, they could only look on helplessly while he drowned. One man had tried to reach out with a walking stick, but the boy failed to grasp it and sank.

Was the sound I heard of children crying in the night a spirit recording of their final cries?

A year later and another tragedy unfolded when a young man met his death by drowning in the cataract, believed to be suicide.

Another death within cooee of the cottage.

Another opportunity for morbid curiosity seekers to visit the site with their rubber necks and their questions.

Apart from long hours in the tollhouse and cramped living conditions, I could understand why Martha had eventually packed up and moved her family to a new locality. Her husband had been keen to try his luck as a woodcutter and move closer to his family on the west coast and with only the three youngest children at home they had hoped for a less hectic lifestyle. Sadly this wasn't to be. Peter had been accidentally killed by a runaway horse just two years later, leaving her a widow with two children still under ten.

Unlucky Martha.

This tragedy had driven her back to the cottage as the only means of providing for her family. Her eldest son, named Peter after his father, became caretaker of the grounds and Martha resumed her place in the toll booth.

They had barely settled in when tragedy struck for a second time. It had been a cold winter day when, with the toll gate closed, Martha took a pail of hot broth to her son who was working nearby. The wind gusted as she turned a corner on the uphill slope and she lost her footing, crashing heavily against the railing, hot liquid splashing her face and hands. Her cries for help went unheard above the roar of the rapids and, realising she needed to get up and moving before hyperthermia set in, she reached out to grasp the railing for support. A fresh wave of pain pulsed as the burns on her palms met the ice covered metal and she moved position to use the crook of her elbow for leverage, pushing down hard on her left leg to raise herself. She stopped to catch her breath when she reached kneeling position, willing herself to find the energy to rise to her feet. Hooking both arms over the top rail she put all her weight into the effort to rise, reaching a half standing position before she felt the outward movement of the barrier before it catapulted her into the greedy river below.

This last information had been unexpected as I hadn't thought before now how Martha had come to her own death, seeing her more as a living entity. This knowledge shocked me in a way I couldn't define, almost like the news of the unexpected death of a close friend, and I decided to finish up for the day.

I had been so engrossed in reading I had forgotten about my bruised knee until I tried to stand, when a combination of cramp and pain almost brought me crashing to the floor until, like Martha, I reached out for support. Fortunately for me, the arm rest of the chair proved substantial enough to hold my weight, saving me from another fall. Moving slowly, it took a while to get the joint working, but at least it held.

The rain had stopped for the moment and I was surprised to see it was almost dark outside and time to think about dinner. I didn't want to face the kitchen again, but eating out meant negotiating the steep steps, my knee jabbing with each step, and I knew I couldn't chance it. I thought of take-out options for home delivery, even going as far as looking up numbers and jabbing in the first few digits before the vulnerability of my position of isolation stilled my thumb. Paranoid perhaps, but I didn't want to advertise the fact I was alone in this secluded place and besides, I couldn't imagine any business delivering to this out of the way place.

I braved the kitchen and settled for two minute noodles, consoling myself with the promise of a walk to the cliff grounds and a decent meal as soon as my knee allowed, where I'd find a corner table at the tea rooms to work, away from the distractions of my mind.

I had never minded being alone, often preferring my own company for long periods, but at that moment I would have loved nothing more than to hear the sound of another voice. I would have like it more if it was someone with knowledge of the cottage or history of the area, someone who could put things in perspective and tame my overactive imagination.

Looking at the situation in this context, I could almost laugh at myself. What had I been thinking, having dream-state arguments and being frightened by every small sound. The cottage was over a hundred years old. The gorge had been in its current form, give or take a rock or two, for many millions of years, and the river had flowed long enough to show the tide levels of the ages. The splashing of water over rocks and fish leaping in the moonlight was all part of the ambience of the gorge, part of the experience of the residency. I needed to immerse myself in it, rein in the research and get down to work.

With this resolve, I went to bed with a lighter heart,

optimistic about what the next day might bring.

Pain in my knee woke me some hours later. Pain, and the deep quiet I was learning to associate with the gorge on windless, rainless nights. Raising my leg I felt an ease of pressure against my foot, similar to the experience of the previous night, and I heard the soft thud of something hitting the floor.

A pillow?

Not likely. Both were firmly under my head.

My robe?

No. I had hung that over the back of one of the armchairs to dry out.

Telling myself it had been too loud to be a spider and too soft to be a rat, I put it down to the doona scraping the floor when I had turned over in bed and reminded myself of my recent resolve to be at one with the cottage.

The clock blinked 4.10. Too early to get up, or was time of any importance living here on my own? There was no one to disturb. No one to mumble about lights turned on or toilets flushed. No sleep quota to meet before an alarm clock deadline, just the luxury of pleasing myself. I had served my time in paid employment, getting up at some ungodly hour to fit in the tasks of the day before battling peak hour traffic into the city. While all that was behind me now, with my former husband unhappily settled with his newer model wife and demands of a young family, and the children of our marriage both living and working abroad, old habits die hard and I had yet to adjust to my retirement from the workforce. Early rising was a compulsion of the industrious that I was trying to shake off.

As if on cue with my waking, the house began to stir with whispers and thumps, grumblings and laughter, all of which I ignored in keeping with my newly formed determination to dispense with paranoia. Deciding to put my imagination to better use in writing and needing to use the bathroom, the decision to get up had been made for me.

I had no feelings of defiance of potential conflict when I entered the kitchen, although I did tread with more care down the small step. This was partly in deference to my knee which still had trouble deciphering the signals from the brain and also from not knowing the physical aspects of the house, or if the roof had a leak I couldn't detect, or condensation that dripped and pooled during the night. The walls had disappeared into themselves as before and I put this down to poor waking vision and the dim light from the low wattage bulb, making a mental note to purchase brighter ones the next time I went into town.

The making of coffee proceeded without incident and I spent the next couple of hours in a frenzy of writing, dashing thoughts down before they disappeared or replaced by others of lesser value. The murmurings of the house continued, interspersed with splashes from the river and the cries of children, poor dead children in their watery graves and their mothers wailing their grief. I absorbed it all into my work, not stopping to question the source or even the rationality of the sounds. They were part of the fabric of the house, as was I, for the moment.

Rather than being tired from my early start, I felt invigorated, liberated by each word that grew to a line and the turning of a page. This was what it was all about. It had taken me a while but I was on my way now.

Mary

They said my death was a wilful case of suicide after my body had been found floating in the South Esk by a fisherman hauling up anchor off the Cataract Mill. I'll leave it to you to make up your own mind.

I lived with my husband of four months in Wellington Street where he was a sweetmeat maker. His mistress of eighteen years also lived in the house and this was the problem, as he had told me when we wed that he'd finished with her. He was a liar as well as a brute who only married me for the money he thought I had. The night before my death he was at me again, cutting most my clothes off me and holding the razor to my throat. I was in fear of my life and ran to my neighbour's house and she took me in and lent me clothes to cover myself. Her husband, on seeing my dishevelled state of undress and blackened eye barred my husband from entering the house, threatening to beat him if he persisted on trying to force his way through the doorway where he stood yowling like a mad creature in his rage. They knew of my husband's temper and had seen me before with bruising and black eyes from his fists. My neighbour escorted me to the corner as I had decided to go to my mother's place in nearby Elizabeth Street.

I knew he'd still be after me and didn't want to take this trouble to my mother's house so I back tracked up the side of the creek. This is when I heard him behind me, raging and threatening to kill me and I ran blind until he caught me on the bridge. My husband told police I had tried to jump off the bridge several times before and had been restrained, but he was unable to verify this as it was a lie.

The coroner found my death was due to drowning but he'd been unable to say how I got in the river, therefore he ruled out suicide. I know I won't rest until I tell my side of the story. Martha said it will happen soon.

Chapter 7

Three days of not moving from the cottage left me slightly stir crazy. My knee had lost most of the swelling and I was ready to face the world again. Reversing the order of the plans I had made the night before, I opted for a leisurely café breakfast at Trevallyn, taking the steep bluestone steps that ran from Kings Bridge on the cottage side of the gorge. I had only gone a short distance when my knee, despite an improvised pressure bandage, began to complain. But by this time I was hooked on the view, stopping frequently to rest and take in the surrounds. This was a magical place of timelessness, of ancient trees and vegetation that thrived in summer humidity and winter rains. I remembered it well from my childhood, when a sense of adventure overtook common sense and I had taken this route instead of the more gradual walk up the road.

The track had offered respite from an unrelenting sun in the summer and there was always the reward of the descent once the summit had been reached after the hard slog up the final path and steps to South Esk Road with its offbeat two step, one step, rhythm.

It was only the promise of respite to come that kept me going once I had reached the halfway mark, the point of no return, where I stopped to rest and looked down on the roof of the cottage. It seemed so high up from the water line when viewed from ground level, when observed from this height if appeared almost as one with the river. I could make out stones of varying sizes on the roof and wondered whether these had been thrown by hand or from the parent rock in times of movement. Smaller tree branches added to the thatch and gave some explanation of the noises I heard at night. I suspected they could also be heard during the day if I listened hard enough, although there were many competing sounds once the city came to life each morning. Traffic from the bridges and the patter of joggers, the chatter of walkers and calls from the tourist launches created a different atmosphere, one of contemporary living far from the hints of yesteryear that came with the fall of night.

The uphill walk served to exercise my knee back to a more usable form and I covered the distance to the café in a quarter to the time it had taken me to climb the steps. Or perhaps the thought of real, café style coffee served as an analgesic.

The coffee shop wasn't far from my childhood home, although it was a very different place these days. Swank, upmarket and trendy would best describe what had once been the sixties style chemist shop, but the staff were friendly enough. The length of my walk meant I had arrived ahead of the lunch time regulars, and the young barista had time for a casual chat between customers. I had probably gone to school with her grandmother and I did some quick mental calculations, deciding if her mother and grandmother had both had teenage pregnancies, as had been the norm in those gender role specific days, then it was a possibility. I didn't ask any questions. Clare Towns may have been mildly curious, Francesca Ashbury didn't need to know.

It was pleasant sitting in the sun, reminiscing with myself about what had been and what may have been and mulling over the easiest way to get to the tearooms, but I couldn't sit there all day. My initial plan to walk up the path from the cottage wasn't feasible now, as this would entail a walk or bus trip back to the bridge and the temptation to put it off once I reached the cottage. Another option would be to take the back road past the primary school, a distance of at least three kilometres, which I didn't think I could manage after the hike I'd already undertaken. In the end I got a taxi, a short fare for the driver that saved a long walk for me. I intended to spend most of the afternoon working from my tablet, if in internet range, or just writing in general.

Some say spring is the best time to visit the cataract, others prefer the shady retreat in summer, or the colour of autumn. I preferred winter when there were less people and mysticism was at its deepest in the ground hugging mist, when gravel paths held and puddled footprints until the next walker came along and the overhanging boughs of evergreens dripped a scented blessing on shoulders as they passed. The screech of peacocks is at its most melancholy in winter, a haunting echo linking past and present. It was a sound like no other that fuelled imagination, like the shriek of a kitten in distress or the cry of a child in the night.

And therein lay the answer to my night noises. I had forgotten the peacocks had been a permanent fixture of the gorge for as long as I could remember. It is strange how the night mind can take something logical and turn it into something else entirely and I was sure I'd sleep better that night with this realisation.

The old tearooms had been transformed as a fine dining restaurant, without losing its original style and charm. The grounds were immaculately kept, with a grassed area that seemed to never reach the rangy stage of my lawn at home. It was truly the place of artists and poets. It was also a place of solitude and meditation, but definitely not for the melancholic, offering as it did a short walk to eternal peace for those of troubled mind and heart.

It was the perfect place for me to collect my thoughts and review what I had written to date. I had been right in my assumption of an unreliable internet connection and had come with fully charged tablet and a folder of notes. My initial plan for the residency had been to write a novel set in the gorge in a contemporary context, however, my recent research had added another dimension to this, broadening to include reference to the past, to the history of the place and its people.

I had developed an interest in the women of the cataract, those who had worked alongside their husbands in the caretaker's cottage, putting in long hours on the gate while keeping house and raising a family, and those poor souls whose lives had been sacrificed to the river. Added to this there had been the everyday events of the gorge and the not so usual happenings that brought pedestrian traffic of a different kind. There had been the thrill seekers and the just plain stupid, who risked their lives for a few minutes of fame, esteemed visitors and royalty, all drawn to the majesty of this place. I could understand them all, even the thrill seekers for, in my youth, I had scaled the southern cliff face with no concern for my safety or anyone else's.

I wanted to get inside the skin of these women. To share their experiences, to understand life in the shadow of the rocks, far beyond what I might experience during my short stay. I wanted to absorb early post-convict Launceston, to understand the adversities and life in the shadow of the quarry that once dominated the lives of so many unfortunates. All of this fell within the criteria of the residency, to create works, ideas, and undertake research relating to the cottage or the Cataract Gorge Reserve in general, and I allowed new concepts to develop, even as I transcribed my notes into a more cohesive form.

Apart from a break after lunch, when I walked down to

the barrier that now denied entry to the river's edge to stretch my legs and declutter my mind, I worked on throughout the afternoon from a table that looked out across the grass to the ferns and rhododendrons beyond. Peacocks, those Beau Brummells of the avian world, strutted their vanity and peahens scuttled after them like submissive housewives grateful for attention. I had introduced myself to the restaurant manager, Louise, explaining the purpose of my visit and she had generously offered the use of a table whenever I wanted. A log fire crackled in the grate and thoughts of Levi were far from my mind.

It was the off season for tourism and, although the venue was popular with the locals, Louise was confident they could accommodate me on any day of my choosing. A member of a local writing group, she had a keen understanding of the needs and mind of the writer and invited me to their meeting the following week. I reciprocated by inviting her and members of her group to the next workshop at the cottage.

Not wanting to overstay my welcome, I packed up just after four and began the walk home along the cliff path, almost deserted at this hour apart from a few joggers running singly or in noisy pairs, yelling to each other between gasps as they passed. Always dark on this side of the river, I was aware of the fading light and hurried my steps as much as the nag in my knee, which had returned on rising after sitting for so long, would allow. I wanted to be back at the cottage before darkness obscured the steps. There had always been a threatening presence in this area, where the curves in the path stretched out over water that reached upwards with sinewy brown arms, as if to grab the unsuspecting. There was one particular area known for the number of suicides where I always increased my pace until I passed. Some years earlier, a woman had taken her two children to this area and thrown the younger one over before the other child understood what was happening. She ran for her life back toward town, looking back only once to see her mother launch herself onto the rocks below. I could never pass this spot with imagining the sheer terror of the child as she ran and I skirted past, almost hugging in the damp rock face to keep as far from the edge rail as possible, noting the bitumen path had worn away in this spot leaving a gap large enough for someone, certainly a child, to slip through. Was this woman one of those who sought Martha's protection in the cottage and was it her child who cried in the night for her mother?

I didn't like entering a darkened house. I never had. There was something almost malevolent about going into a gloomy space, when no light had been left burning or warm fire to crackle welcome. I liked the idea of a candle in the window, but I didn't think the council insurance would cover this.

My legs were tired. Muscles unused to walking long distances reminded me of my sedentary lifestyle, although my knee had coped well with the exertion considering the hike that morning. I had favoured it since the fall, when I should have carried on past the pain and it would have whipped itself into shape earlier. I had hit my head at the same time and probably with more force, yet I had shown it no favours and just got on with my work and, apart from tenderness when brushing my hair, there had been no lingering effects. A warm bath would take care of the aching muscles, then a light supper in front of the heater before turning in for the night. Sometimes exhaustion brought its own rewards.

But fatigue, while bringing sleep, proved insufficient to keep me asleep for the whole night and I was wide awake staring at the clock at just after three. I punched into the pillow and pulled the darkness over me, eventually falling into a fitful sleep before succumbing to full wakefulness an hour later. As on other nights, the voices from the kitchen grew in volume, the angry banging of pans, the cries of the children and voices of anxious mothers. I had wanted to get to know the women of the cottage, but this regular intrusion into my dreams hadn't been what I had in mind.

Loudest of all was the incessant howling of an infant who refused to be shushed; peacocks calling into the night.

There appeared to be some sort of dispute and I lay still as their words carried through the wall.

'I say we tell her.'

'What on earth for?'

'Because she may be able to help find the mother.'

'Don't be stupid woman. Her mother's long gone.'

'She has to be somewhere.'

'You don't get it, do you? And if she found this mother, what of the others? No, I've seen to them all these years and I'll decide when it's time to go.'

'But the baby cries for her ma.'

As if on cue the infant's cries became louder, a pleading desperation in the tiny voice as she called her mournful cry.'

'Mama! Mama!'

'Look what you've done now. You've set her off again. Shush little one. Come sit on Martha's knee. There, there, that's better now, isn't it?'

The cries subsided to a low blubber and the conversation continued as before. Saucepans banged and teacups rattled as a background to the women's conversation and I strained to hear what they were talking about.

'I still think we should speak to her. She's the only one in all these years who's shown any interest.'

'Sticking her nose in where it's not wanted. How's that taking an interest?'

'You're too harsh, Martha. You invited her to speak then you refused to listen to her.'

'Rubbish, and you heard her laughing at us with the other women.'

'What I do know is it's about time the children, and all of us, continued our journey. Anyway, it's not only you who has a say in this. It's not just your cottage, Martha, not really. '

There followed the sound a chair scraping against wooden floor and a dull thud of something dropping and a child's yelp of surprise before the howling started afresh, more loudly this time.

'Mama! I want my mama!'

'Oh, look what you've done now. Be off with you child and you can stop that noise as well.'

I heard the sound of a slap and the patter of running feet fading into the distance.

'I'm telling you, Gertie, you need to mind your own business or else who knows what will happen to any of us. I've been put out once before you know, and look what happened then.'

'I know, Martha, I know, but I'd like to go home again one day.'

'You are home for the moment, woman, so stop your nonsense and get on with it.'

I needed to break the pattern of rising in the early hours of the morning only to nod off during the day and, with a workshop to conduct in a few hours, I needed to at least sound as if I knew what I was talking about. These waking dreams, for my mind refused to accept any other explanation for the visitations, were becoming a bit too much and I wasn't about to cede control to these disembodied voices of the night. Apart from a slight raising of hair on the back of my neck, I wasn't that afraid of the supernatural. My experience with

Levi had taught me there was so much more to fear from the living than the dead.

Pulling the doona over my ears, I meditated once again on jumping sheep until sleep returned.

Gertrude

Before my death I had been the organist and Sunday School teacher at St. Paul's Church, helping my father when I was able. I had problems from time to time. They called it a mental aberration, or dyspeptic hysteria, a disturbance of the digestive system.

I was twenty-four years of age and well into spinsterhood when I died. My health was poor and I feared a return of a severe illness of a more aggravated character, knowing it could prostrate me for some months and I'd be sent away for a change of scene and climate until I became well again. In the week before my demise I began to manifest a return of symptoms that left me wholly unfitted for my usual domestic occupations, or from taking any interest in them, due to the frequent severe fits of despondency that attended these. I felt there was little to live for.

I told my father I was going to a friend's house for tea and would not be at choir practice that evening as I didn't feel well enough to play the organ, the duties of which I had regularly discharged when in good health. He began to worry when I hadn't returned by ten o'clock and made some enquiries as to my whereabouts without success. He then made search for me the whole night through, but failed to learn anything until shortly after six that morning. He'd just returned home when he received a message requesting him to go up to the reservoir at Cataract Hill where my body had been found.

The doctor had cautioned my father to be vigilant, as

another attack might cause temporary insanity, but I knew what I intended to do and I had planned it with precision. Kitting myself with chloroform and brandy to bring about my death, I made my way to the reservoir above the river, removing palings to gain access to the enclosure. I took off my gloves, scarf and watch, placing these inside my hat with the vial once I had emptied its contents. Drinking deeply of the brandy to steady my nerves, I then saturated a handkerchief with the chloroform and placed this over my face, holding my breath until I had knotted it behind my head. From there it was only a few deep inhalations until peace descended.

There were some who didn't believe I had done this myself and that I had been the victim of foul play, so hard had it been for them to accept the truth. This had been, in part, due to the abrasion on my forehead that came about when I slipped after taking the brandy and hit my head on the concrete.

I had thought about drinking the chloroform but decided against this as, with my unruly stomach, there was always the chance I'd vomit and lose my chance of death. There can be no doubt that, while in a state of temporary insanity occasioned by severe mental and bodily depression, I had caused my own demise. But nothing is ever as simple or as black and white as that. There's always the back story and once this has been told, I can join my parents in heaven.

Chapter 8

Entering the kitchen the next morning I narrowly avoided slipping on the wet floor, grabbing the sink to stop my fall as I began to slide. I was thinking this was becoming something of a habit, when I noticed there were several wet patches on the boards with nothing to account for their presence. The ceiling was dry, with no apparent condensation, the small window, although not draught proof, was latched shut, and it hadn't rained during the night that I was aware of. I'd have to report it to Jana. I didn't want to, however, there could be a problem with the plumbing. Although I hadn't noticed one when I had been on the steps the day before, if there was a header tank for the hot water tank on the roof or in the ceiling cavity, and it had a fault, I didn't want it to get worse on my watch. For now a mop up with a towel would have to suffice and I'd phone Jana when I returned to the cottage in the afternoon.

I had been looking forward to the day's activity, more interactive exercise than workshop, at a nearby school. I had conducted a few sessions at different alternative schools around Victoria and their unconventional educational approach, characterized by an emphasis on independence, freedom within limits and respect for a child's natural development, translated into interested and interesting participants at each event. I anticipated today would be no different. Even better, it was within easy walking distance on the opposite hill.

What I hadn't foreseen was my own reaction to *Arches College of Alternative Education*, an imposing Victorian mansion set high on the hill. Dignified in its restored state, it somehow lacked the warm welcome I had been expecting, despite the laughter and chatter of children coming from the rear of the property. This feeling of foreboding eased with the greeting called from the front veranda when Alice, a young woman I recognised from a workshop I had attended the previous week for younger writers, called down to me. I hadn't realised she had been a student from this school as it had been an evening function. Working with young people was something I most enjoyed, the passing on of skills and knowledge to others, learning more myself in the process.

In response to questions I asked about the house and its history, Alice offered to give me a guided tour, as she had written a paper on its history the previous year.

Built as a family home in 1881, for the Warden for the Launceston Marine Board, on what had then been a smallholding, it passed to a religious organisation in 1900 who ran it as a home for unmarried mothers. After its closure in 1960 it had been used as a boarding house, then a guest house, before the current owners purchased the rundown property in 1995 and opened the school.

The high ceilinged rooms were colourful, with details of ornate plaster work highlighted in pastels and gilding, giving the impression of lightness, however, I detected the residue of shadows in corners and some rooms had a chill that no amount of bright paint or sunlight would eradicate. It was an atmosphere synonymous with the hills and valleys of the city. Alice was a perfunctory guide and I had the impression she had given this tour so many times she had committed it to memory, with most of her information centreing on its time as a home for unmarried mothers.

'And this was the office where the girls were interviewed when they first arrived,' she paused and looked straight at me before continuing, 'it was also the room where they handed their babies over to the people who adopted them.'

Her voice was a mixture of challenge and judgement, although her face remained as before, pleasant yet impassive. I was unable to discern whether her judgement was against the unfortunate girls or those who took their babies from them, or whether the challenge was against me or some anonymous authority. We walked up the rather grand staircase to the first floor, where several doors opened from a central landing, all now used as various subject rooms except for one, smaller than the rest, which stood empty.

'What's this room for?' I asked as she whisked me past the door.

'We don't use it for anything these days because no one likes going in there. Bad vibes and all that.'

My expression of interest wasn't returned, so I pushed a little harder, sensing a story idling in the empty space, 'and why is that do you think?'

'We don't like to talk about it either. It's just a feeling you get when you go inside.'

Even standing on the threshold of the room, I could sense what she wasn't saying. A definite presence chilled the air and had begun a slow crawl up the back of my neck.

'Do you know any history of this particular room?'

'Not really. It had been a maid's room when the original family lived here, then it was nursery when it was a maternity home, where babies were kept until they could be adopted,' her voice became sharper as offered this information, 'and after that I think it was just a bedroom. We don't worry about it too much and the door's usually kept locked.'

Her mood lightened once we moved away and she became more animated when discussing programs run by the school and the benefit she and other students derived from these, adding amusing anecdotes to illustrate her tales. I could see the future writer in her animation and in her use of language. By the time we reached the classroom I had forgotten the room upstairs and was ready to return to work.

Today I had planned a more serendipitous approach to the session, much as a sailor sets the tiller on autopilot, yet always at hand should the vessel veer too far off course. The students were eager to learn and show their story writing ability and I thought how much they could teach older writers in opening their minds to the infinite ideas that exist around us and the flexibility of language used to in show this to the reader. Scheduled as a morning activity, the informal curriculum and timetable allowed us to stop for lunch and resume in the afternoon if all were in agreement.

During the morning, which had focussed on poetry, many students had chosen to write about their immediate surroundings so I expanded on that during the afternoon in the writing of short stories. They wrote fast and with vigour I was envious of, some writing longhand and others tapping away on notebooks, stopping only occasionally to ask me to clarify a point of grammar or format. The results of the day's writing would be produced as a book to be sold as part of the school's annual fundraising and all were eager for my comment at the end of the day. I asked each student to assess their own work and give me their best to take away and read at my leisure, promising to return these with my comments by the end of the week.

I didn't want to place too much pressure on myself, but I also didn't want unfinished tasks hanging over my head when I still had to firm up the first draft of my own novel. Some handed me poems, while others gave me stories of varying lengths. Alice was the last to hand hers in and I noticed it was considerably longer than the others, about twenty pages at a glance. I had been right about her natural talent as a writer.

Because of the extended time of the workshop, it was late afternoon when I arrived back at the cottage. Had it been any season other than winter there would have been several hours of daylight left in which to walk to the shops, as it was, darkness was already creeping into the rooms, chasing out the last of the light. I dropped the Roman blinds into position and turned on the lights and the TV. Apart from the news and a few good British dramas, I didn't watch much television and my plan had been to have a relaxed early dinner while watching the news and then make a start reading the students' work after that. It was too late to phone the council about the water leak and, anyway, the floor was bone dry now so maybe I wouldn't need to bother them.

What happened next was illogical and I say that because it occurred when I was at my most relaxed, not hungry or tired or under any other physical stress. I had finished my meal and was watching the local news reporter following a feel good story in a Launceston street when I saw a familiar face in the crowd.

Levi.

I'd know him anywhere. He wasn't averse to adopting different roles to suit an occasion and I had seen expansive changes to his demeanour when playing the victim in court, but with his level of arrogance and narcissism he'd see no reason to radically alter his physical appearance in any way. Why would he, when he firmly believed in his own power and privilege and his right to destroy others for what his persecution complex convinced him were slights against.

My heart hammered in my chest, breath coming in pants as I struggled against the physical aspects of fear, while voices in my mind argued with each other.

'It wasn't him, stupid. It's just someone who looks like

him.'

'It was him. I know it was. He's found out where I am. It's all been for nothing.'

'Don't be stupid. How could he possibly know? He doesn't even know your new name.'

'It was him. It was.'

Backward and forward it went until I was a blithering mess, huddled in my chair in a corner where I could see every wall and access to the room, while common sense affirmations from previous therapy sessions twanged in and out of the mix.

Even if it had been him, and the calm of passing time told me it probably hadn't been, because he couldn't possibly know where I was. I'd only had a glance at someone in the crowd, a flash, and it was most likely one feature of that person that triggered my reaction. He didn't know my new name, I was sure of that. I had covered my path too well over an extended period of time. And my appearance had changed. I had lost almost half my previous body weight. I no longer dyed my hair, allowing the grey to take over and wearing it in a more grandmotherly cap. Contact lenses had given way to black rimmed glasses, and I was older now, so much older than the passing years would suggest; another legacy of Levi.

It had just been a panic attack. It happened now and then, often for no reason I could see and it was better to forget about it rather than drive myself crazy with what ifs.

I settled back to reading the students' work, most of it so good it only required words to this effect and comments for them to reflect on. The stories took a little longer than the poetry, yet even these were of such a high standard I had little to offer by way of suggestion for change. These kids were good and this said a lot for alternative schooling. It's amazing what you get if you don't try to hammer a child into a mould that's not of their fit, something state education and many private schools, with their over-reliance on rules and regulations have never really grasped. Give a child freedom to grow and learn and they'll find their own unique shape.

I had left Alice's story until last, thinking I might have to hold it over until tomorrow if it became too late, but time was on my side and, probably due to my adrenalin-raising fright earlier, I was still wide awake and not the least bit tired. I had reached the bottom of the first page of her story before I realised my error in not setting it aside. Whereas the other children had written positive poems and stories based on nature and goodness, Alice had written a dark tale of conspiracy and death, so graphic in her description of the misery of life that I was immediately drawn into the story.

I shouldn't have been surprised her story had been set in the school building when it had been a maternity home. I thought about the strange look that had crossed her face during my tour of the house when she had spoken about the past history, and again when I had questioned her about the empty room upstairs. As I read further, I also realised the story hadn't been written during the afternoon session. It was too detailed, too polished, and I wondered at her motive in writing it. If she had wanted an assessment of her writing she could have just asked. It had been made it clear at the beginning of the day that I was open to progressing their writing in whatever manner they chose.

Her story was about Maisie, a young girl who'd had her baby taken for adoption and a week later committed suicide by drowning. It was a story thick with grief and hopelessness and despair so deep the young mother could see no way out other than by death. More than a short story, it was part opinion piece, part editorial, with strong judgements written in the girl's suicide note for those who had stolen her child and utterances of retribution for those who continued the practice of forcibly separating mother and child. The writing was so graphic, I could picture Maisie sitting in that small room holding tight to her baby before it was wrenched from her arms.

It was a fine piece of writing, yet I struggled to think of a possible market for it even amongst the genres covered under dark fiction. I even wondered whether the school authorities, as relaxed as they appeared to be on individual choice, would allow this to be included in their fundraiser book. Still, it wasn't my worry. I made comments as appropriate on character and conflict development, plot and theme, and decided not to remark on the setting at all.

Satisfied with a productive day and evening's work and having put my earliest fears about Levi to rest, I was confident of an undisturbed night's sleep. I lifted the blind to the side as I walked toward the bedroom to see the moon refracting off on the churning river and closed my mind to the image of Maisie throwing herself off the cliff onto the rocks below.

Maisie

Life was unkind when I was young, with harsh social attitudes and judgements for those who broke the moral code. I was naïve in the manner of youth, and thought I had all the answers, until I had to tell Peter I was having a baby. I expected he'd be shocked and then take charge as he did in all things and we'd get married quietly and move into respectability. It didn't happen. Oh, he was shocked all right, so stunned his parents spirited him away to another state and I was left to face the shame on my own. Without a family to turn to, my landlady took one look at my growing belly and arranged for me to go into the home on the hill. The place people only spoke about in whispers. The place where bad girls went to hide their disgrace.

Even after he left I still had hope. He loved me, I was sure of that, and I blamed his parents for his absence, believing he'd be back before the child was born and we'd be together as planned. All I had ever wanted was a family of my own, someone to belong to, to love and be loved in return. I'd hold my stomach and send love through to my baby, promising we would be together forever.

Forever turned out to be a few short weeks. Peter never returned and they said I had to give my baby, a little girl I called Claire, away to a good home. I argued and cried and refused to sign the papers, all to no avail, as they told me I had signed when I first entered the home. I had no memory of this and knew they were lying but what could I do? I had no home to take a baby to and they said if I tried to keep her they would call welfare and they'd take her anyway. I was heartbroken. I cried for a week after they'd prised her from my arms and then I knew what I had to do. I couldn't live without my baby. I had loved her for nine months in my womb and, if I thought about it, I had loved the thought of her for most of my life, of having a warm body to love and to hold. Now she was gone and there was no hope for me.

The day they put me out of the home I walked over the hill to the cataract and once I reached the edge of the rock face I walked into air and into the water. As the water closed over me I felt my earthly pain disappear, finding myself surrounded by other lost souls and children nobody had wanted. I try to love them, but they're not Claire and I need to tell her she was loved always and forever. Lately I've been hearing her calling my name as I've called out to her, but I'm still searching.

Chapter 9

I was right in expecting an undisturbed sleep, although I misjudged the length of the night by several hours, waking to the illumination of the clock flashing at 3.39. The house was quiet. No conversation from the kitchen or children crying for their mothers, which just went to show it had been the wind all along. The wind and my anxiety ridden imagination. I turned over and tried to make it easier for sleep to find me, but my mind stayed several steps ahead, thinking disconnectedly about Levi, Alice's story, the cottage, and character development for my novel.

Of course it would be too much to expect my imagination not to hike up another notch or two and my hypersensitive hearing to pick up the slightest sound from outside. It didn't let me down. As if on cue I heard the crackle of a twig underfoot followed by a heavy scrape, the sort made by someone with a limp where one leg doesn't have the height lift of the other. My mind went immediately to Levi. He hadn't had a limp I was aware of, yet I knew once he stepped into a role he the capacity to take on all physical aspects of the personality of his creation, or he could have had an injury since the last time I had seen him. I thought back to the news cast.

Had he limped?

How much could the mind absorb in a flash?

Had it even been Levi that I saw?

Panic, never far from my side, rose dramatically, my breath coming in shallow pants, each exhale a plea to an unhearing god. The knowing part of my mind could see the situation for what it was, an anxiety attack, but my prey mentality was poised to attention and the two sides squabbled in head, splitting with ferocity as if I was merely the spectator to my own fate. I made efforts to intervene, to slow my thoughts to a level where reason could resume control, only to have this superseded by another sound outside the window and the silent scream of terror rose another notch.

And I lay there in this panicked state, listening, alert, until the first whisper of dawn framed the sides of the blind. Only then did my muscles relax enough to allow movement, to do what I should have done when I first woke, and I reached for the packet of Alprazolam I had been avoiding since my arrival in Launceston. They belonged to the person I had once been, not Francesca Ashbury, and I had hoped I could beat the anxiety by using strategies suggested by Marcus. This time it wasn't enough. The little blue pill and a strong coffee would right my world.

Whether from the medication taking effect or the fuller force of daylight, a sense of calm returned, bringing common sense with it, and I took my coffee into the back yard to investigate the source of the noises that set off the panic attack. A few broken twigs that had snapped off the trees higher on the cliff lay scattered on the pavers while, closer to the window, a plastic bag had wandered in on a draft to become caught on the frayed edge of a weatherboard. Even as I watched, a barely perceptible breeze lifted it slightly and it dragged against the window frame.

Walking around to the side of the house where the latch gate opened at the top of the steps, there was nothing to show there'd been any human presence other than my own. Imagination and a fragile nervous system were not the bedfellows I needed and I resolved once more to take greater control of my thoughts before they spun out of control.

Taking advantage of this sense of wellbeing, I managed to pound out a couple of thousand words before they petered out. As with most of my writing, this novel had been founded on fact, about an unsolved murder and a missing body and the impact of this on a city unused to crime of this nature. I had set out to write the story as general fiction, however, it had begun to take on a life of its own as the protagonist, an amateur sleuth, set out to solve the crime. First he had to find the body, and that's where I became stuck and white page syndrome set in, that curse of all writers where blank paper meets bank mind.

I tossed up between taking a nap or going for a walk and the latter won. With more rain forecast for the remainder of the week I needed to get out while I had the chance and, with this in mind, I decided to return the students' work and that would be one less thing to worry about. I had enjoyed the walk the day before and thought to vary this by looping back through town on my way home where I could pick up something for dinner and a bottle of wine as a reward for the progress I had made. A quick phone call to the school to make sure someone would be around to take receipt of the folder and I was off.

The steps leading down to the cliff path always took careful navigation, the uneven rocks had trip potential and mossy growth created a slippery surface for the unsure of foot. I kept my eyes down to circumvent disaster and that was how I noticed the cigarette butts, three of them butted out against the rock side wall and dropped carelessly onto the steps. My mind began the old pattern of slipping into paranoiac suspicion before my resolve to control rather than be controlled slipped in. Obviously the alcove of the steps had been used by someone waiting to meet another and they'd had a couple of cigarettes to pass the time. Not everything had to have a sinister motive and I had forgotten about the butts by the time I reached the toll booth that marked the end of the path, or the beginning, depending on which direction you were going.

On the other side of the booth, three arched alcoves provided shelter for ancient wooden bench seats bolted to the rock face, uninviting even in the daylight, as the warmth of the sun never reached inside the recess. I hadn't liked the area when I had been a child and the years hadn't made them any more welcoming. Urinous, dark, dank and foreboding, I couldn't imagine anyone choosing to rest in there. Alternatively, it made an excellent hiding place for anyone not wishing to be seen, unlit as it was by day and by night.

Alice met me at the bottom of the drive leading up to the school, fidgeting, eyes darting. I had the feeling she had been waiting for me.

'Did you read my story?' She didn't waste any time on niceties.

'Yes. I've read all the work students wrote yesterday. You're a talented group.'

'And what did you think of mine?'

'I thought it was very well written, so much so that I wondered if you'd written it all yesterday or if it was something you'd started before then.'

'No, I wrote it yesterday, although I've been thinking about it for a long time – a very long time.'

'It was a different subject, compared to the other students, that is.'

'I am different.'

We'd slowed our steps, coming to a stop near a garden bench halfway up the drive and Alice sat as if to emphasise her difference.

'Well, we're all different aren't we? All made in our own special way.'

She ignored this and went on as if I hadn't spoken, 'Did you like my story though? Not the writing but the story itself?'

I was about to say no, but stopped myself in the nick of time because that wasn't true. I hadn't disliked the story at all. What I hadn't liked so much was the underlying anger that permeated the words, almost as a challenge to the reader to dare hold an opinion of their own.

'The story was interesting and I did wonder what the genesis for it was, where the idea came from, and how much of it was fiction and how much came from your research into the school building.'

'But how much of fiction is truly fiction anyway?' She glanced at me as if to gauge my reaction. 'Didn't you tell us yesterday that every story began with a grain of truth, the seed that grows through nurture by the creative mind?'

'Yes, I did say that and it's true. It's just that I felt your story was more about real people and events, belonging more to the genre of speculative nonfiction rather than fiction. Not that it matters, because you were all invited to write according to personal choice and that meant we ended up with a mix of genres, which will make for great reading when the book is published.'

'Oh, they won't use my story.'

'Why on earth not? The writing is excellent and they're sure to want to use it. It's also longer than the other students' work and this will add balance to the layout of the anthology.'

'They won't put it in because we're not supposed to talk about what went before. That's why I wrote it as fiction, but if you could see it's based on truth, and you don't really know anything about the place, then others will pick it up.'

'We'll see. I'll be speaking with the principal about the work when I drop these off and suggesting they use your story as the first entry.'

Standing up as suddenly as she'd sat down a few minutes earlier, she took a few steps before turning back to me, 'Can I have my story back please? I've decided I don't want it in the book after all.'

'But it's a wonderful piece of writing…'

'Sorry, I'm just not ready to share it. Not yet anyway.'

Now I was the uncertain one, wondering how the school would react to the missing work or if they'd even notice. Certainly there'd been no supervision by school staff over what the students produced or any count of items I had taken away to read. On the other hand, I didn't know how the system worked and whether there'd be an expectation that all students who participated in the session would produce something at the end of it. As usual when in doubt I followed the line of least resistance and handed the papers to Alice.

'I've written comments in the margins if you're interested, a few suggestions and observations and comments about the work in general.'

'Thank you,' we'd reached a fork in the path where one way led to the front entrance, the other to the back of the property, 'I'll go this way and catch up with the others.'

'Bye then, but think about whether you want to hand in the story. It is good reading.'

She laughed her farewell, a cynical half laugh, and I went in search of Zalie, the principal. The good feelings I had carried from the previous day had dropped a notch, as if I had unwittingly become caught up in a conspiracy that had nothing to do with me and decided I'd say nothing about the missing story unless I was specifically asked about it. When I thought about it later though, I had to admit it was probably for the best that the story didn't make it into the book. It had a negativity to it that wasn't reflected in the other work and the expressed anger made it seem all the more personal. I might have spent more time pondering the secret of the off limits room and the link to the past when I read the story, had I not been so absorbed by my own unfolding novel and nightly survival in the cottage.

Leaving the school, I trekked the steep downhill path to Maitland Street with its strange mix of architecture, from modest weatherboard cottages to an ornate gingerbread house that dominated the street and from there I wound my way through the streets and lanes to Morty's Complex in Brisbane Street. This hadn't been my destination when I had started out earlier, when I had intended to stop at the supermarket for a few supplies, but Morty's offered a range of take outs and I could always shop another day. Meal preparation for one was that easy.

Looking back, this day marked the point where I began to find excuses for being away from the cottage whenever possible although, paradoxically, I confined my absences to daylight hours when I actually felt safest. Nights were the real problem and yet I made sure I was back there, locked in with blinds drawn and lights blazing long before the last rays of light slipped behind the cataract. I refused any further invitations to attend evening events, citing commitment to the novel, painting a picture of myself as a reclusive night writer.

Passing the toll booth, I thought about Martha and the other women who had spent hours each day in the cramped space, taking pennies and threepences from day trippers while their husbands took care of the gardens and amenities within the cliff grounds. It may not have been too bad when the weather was mild and business brisk, but in the extreme heat of summer it would have been unbearable under the tin roof, despite its steep pitch and the narrow veranda around the four sides of the building. Winters would have been worse with no place for a fire and young children to tend to.

It was still daylight, so I had the luxury of time to stop inside the latch gate and take in the view from this aspect. With the narrow yard unadorned by plants or other decoration and bordered by a low picket fence it was reminiscent of a widows walk looking down on the river below. And it may have also served this purpose for women or children looking out for those due home at the end of a long day, or for someone taking time out from the toll booth to tend to their children.

As most pedestrian traffic could be expected to come via the bridge, the narrow space provided an excellent lookout for potential customers, to assess how much time they had before hurrying back to their duty. Even better if they had a child old enough to place on watch while they completed household tasks, a quick cooee if they saw someone approaching and no one would ever know of their absence. How well this would have worked in the winter when pea soup fogs hung around the valley, limiting visibility for a few inches, was anyone's guess. Or maybe the toll only operated at certain times of the year. I made a mental note to explore this further as I entered the cottage and went about the routine tasks of locking the world out.

It had long been my habit to pause at the end of each day to reflect on my activities and the interaction I'd had with other people. It was a way of both signing tasks off and designating others for a future time. While I hadn't done a lot this day, I found plenty to ponder on, not the least Alice withdrawing her story. I hoped I hadn't contributed to her decision by any comment I had made, but I sensed it had been more than that. Her story had been deeply personal and she'd had second thoughts about others picking up on this and possibly asking questions she didn't want to answer. Why couldn't she have just written a poem, even one of a personal nature wouldn't have drawn particular scrutiny. Poetry was like that, a licence that would have allowed her to write whatever she chose.

Adding to my unease was the thought that I was central to her telling the story at this time, that she had wanted me to read it for some reason. Still, there was no point dwelling on it as she was the only one with the answers and I had enough to keep me busy. Books don't write themselves.

There were a few social media commitments requiring attention before I could settle into the evening. Building a writer's platform was important in this new era of publishing, but maintaining this took time, often too much time. I had linked all the accounts set up in my new name, concentrating primarily on blog posts connected to Facebook, Twitter and other social media to keep the momentum of the profile going. However, blogs required regular posts to keep the information current. I had focussed my recent activity on the residency, photos taken on my walks, poems in draft form, or a brief travelogue of sorts with a one line progress report at the end, gaining new followers along the way.

Some blog visitors left comments of encouragement or offered additional information about the area, others messages went straight to the spam folder. For someone of my reclusive nature it was a way of interacting with others at a distance. I had always been reserved in company, and events of recent years had made me distrustful of strangers and forming new acquaintances.

Opening the dashboard for the blog I went straight to comments. With nothing specific in mind to write about, I hoped to gain inspiration from the opinion of others, as sometimes happened, and to build on this. There were five comments left for the previous day's post, two from regular followers and the others from an anonymous poster. Not always a good sign.

My last post had been a poem about life.

> we run
> the marathon of life
> rushing
> toward the finish line
> name etched in marble

Comment 1:
What will the marble say? Evil! I think in your case a timber stake would be enough. Karma follows you to the next life.

Anonymous

The other two comments were in similar vein and been clearly composed by the same person, deeply personal messages of hate that sent a chill straight through me, my imagination spearing into overdrive, the constriction on my chest pushing my breath out in frantic gasps. I'd seen similar messages before and I knew who they were from.

Not again, please God, not again.

It was Levi. It had to be him. He had tracked me down and this was his way of letting me know. The cat and mouse game had resumed.

What should I do?

I stared at the words, hoping I had misread them, looking for some clue, any clue, as to their creator.

The panic attack of this morning returned, my hands were clammy and shaking uncontrollably, the blanket of terror suffocating as my heart raced and nausea paralysed me.

The loss of control was almost total and I struggled to find the inner voice of reason that might steer me back to a point of rational thinking.

Breathe deeply and slowly.

In and out.

In and out.

It's not him. Not Levi. Just some social media troll flexing their spook muscles.

Have an Alprazolam. Have two.

I tried to obey these commands, but my knees had turned to jelly, refusing to hold my weight. The nausea had shifted to my bowels and the physicality of this, and the certain knowledge of what would happen if I didn't move, sent me dropping to the floor and a rapid crawl on all fours to the bathroom.

This almost loss of control reversed the attack enough for me to make my way to the bedroom from the bathroom and snatch the medication from where I had left it that morning. Two tablets washed down by furry water in the bottom of the glass on the bedside table. This used up the last of my energy and I rested against the side of the mattress to wait for the out of body calm that would soon follow.

No thinking, because this could lead back to over-thinking, I needed to find my way to that place of just being.

And I slept.

I woke to find myself in pitch darkness, with cramping in my thighs and a ball of pain where my knees had ground against the wooden floor. It took a minute or two to get my bearings. The panic had gone now and I pushed through the disorientation of the medication to my last waking memory, working backward from the crawl from the sitting room and the frantic scramble to reach the bathroom. I hadn't put the bedroom light on as I had fallen asleep where I had sat on the floor, before slipping onto my side.

The blog comments that precipitated the attack now seemed of little consequence. Anyone could have left them. The internet was full of trolls with nothing better to do than incite debate or instil fear in people they didn't know. The wording of the comments were similar to those used by Levi in the past, but they had been out there for anyone to read and take as their own. I had to stop with the suspicion. I could either turn tail and run, or face the situation head on.

I switched on the bedside lamp and changed position on the floor, not ready yet to try my legs. My heart was beating at its normal pace, hands shaking only spasmodically and the nausea had left me. So effective had the Alprazolam been, all fear of the night cottage and Levi had dulled to nothingness. I'd had double the recommended dose today, which accounted for the disorientation. This, and the fact I had been up since before daylight and had an active day. Feeling relaxed and unafraid seemed too good an opportunity for a solid night's sleep to miss so, kicking off my shoes, I dragged myself onto the bed and slept some more.

Ida

Like so many of us who ended up in the river, the coroner's finding was one of suicide while mentally disturbed. I was not mentally disturbed, nor did I take my own life. I suppose this outcome was easier for the men who sat on the jury as they could only think as men of the time, that women were at best fragile creatures who fell apart at the slightest obstacle. That hadn't been me. I was tough and those who knew me well could have attested to this had they chosen to.

My brother in law, with whom I lived, had warned me against seeing Jim. He didn't like him and didn't want him near his home and this made it difficult for all concerned. I know Jim told the court we only had a pure relationship but he lied about this just as he lied about knowing of my death as we had been intimate for most of the nine months we had been seeing each other. He also lied about us not talking about marriage for we spoke of little else, of getting our own place and settling down.

On the night of my death I met Jim and we lay together under some trees near the Mowbray estate. He didn't want me to go home, but I told him it would cause another row if I didn't so we agreed I should go home at the expected time and go to my room as if going to bed. Then I was to leave quietly by the back door, through the rear gate into the laneway behind the houses and meet him at the end of Gunn Street.

There were so many loose ends in this case I'm surprised any person of intelligence didn't pick up on them. There were the lies told by Jim about our relationship and the untruths told by my brother in law as to the extent of the rancour he held toward James. Even my own dear sister supposedly saying I was going to do away with myself.

Why would she say this when I had never expressed any desire to do so?

Why would my brother in law head straight to the river to find me?

I have the answers to these questions if only Francesca will write my story and then I can finally let go.

Chapter 10

The clock showed 9.35 and I could hear my mobile ringing from the sitting room where I had left it the night before. Not inclined to rush to answer, and knowing it would most probably ring out before I got there, I ignored it and rolled over to enjoy the sensation of sleeping in after an undisturbed sleep, a delicious half consciousness of that in-between place of sleep and wakefulness.

And then the phone rang again and there was no avoiding the day.

'Hello Francesca?' The greeting was by way of a question, a habit shared by many. It was Zalie, the principal of Arches school, 'I hope I'm not disturbing you.'

'No, that's okay,' another phone convention, the habit of the white lie, 'what can I help you with?'

'I'm calling about the students' stories from the other day. I noticed after you'd dropped them off yesterday that Alice's was missing and I wondered if it had accidentally got left behind after you'd read them.'

This wasn't the position I wanted to be in, caught between an adolescent and her intention and the school principal and her purpose.

'No,' I wasn't sure whether to be evasive or simply tell the truth. In the end truth won out, 'I took them all back yesterday, but Alice asked for hers to be returned to her when I met her in the driveway. Perhaps she wanted to edit it some more before it was handed in.'

I didn't think this was the case, but it gave Alice an out if she needed it, although I couldn't see why she'd need to be worried, when the nature and philosophy of the school was about students making their own choices and accepting responsibility for these.

'Oh.' That's all she said. Just, oh.

I felt I'd done something wrong. It didn't take much for guilt and self-doubt to emerge and with this came compulsive apologies. 'I'm sorry. Shouldn't I have given her work back to her when she asked?'

'No, that's all right. We wanted to include something in the anthology from all the students who attended your workshop and I noticed Alice's story was missing.'

'Perhaps if you asked her...'

'What was her story about?' Now I was really uncomfortable. I didn't want to be questioned in this manner over such a paltry matter.'

'Oh, it was a story set in the house, the school building that is... a speculative fiction piece.'

'Not a true story then?'

'I don't think so. No, I'm sure it was just a story she created as part of the exercise.'

'About this school?'

'Yes. Is that a problem?'

'No, not a problem, no. Alice shows great promise as a writer, but she's been fixated on the history of this building for some time now and I was hoping for something different from her.'

'That may be why she took her story back. It could be she intends to submit another one.' I found it hard to believe I was even having this conversation. Zalie had seemed pretty casual when I had met her, not the type to get het up about a student's story, 'I'm sure you'll work it out with her and yes, she does write well.'

I bade her a quick farewell, citing writing commitments, glad to distance myself from what seemed to me to be a storm in a teacup.

An hour later the conversation had all but vanished from my mind, along with the feelings of panic and anxiety that had brought about the meltdown the day before. Once I'd had a shower and breakfast I felt I could do anything I set out to do.

I liked the way the sun came through the study windows on the days when winter allowed it to shine through the cloud cover, although today this wasn't enticement enough to sit at the desk and work. I needed fresh air to chase away the last of the cobwebs and a walk up the cliff path was just the way to achieve this. Thinking I might tackle the zig zag path on the other side, I poked the camera in a side pocket of my bag as added incentive to walk the full circuit. I often used photos or images for ideas when creating a setting for a story and the smaller details of particular environments, the flora and insect life, added authenticity.

There had been a moment the previous night when I had resolved to phone Marcus the minute I woke, to discuss the wisdom of continuing with the residency after the return of the panic attacks, resisting the temptation to call him then and there. A reasonable night's sleep and an almost sunny morning, and probably to a larger extent the anti-anxiety meds in my system, allowed me to see the situation through calmer, less troubled eyes. I knew what the triggers were for me and I needed to avoid these where possible. I understood the complexities of schema and how this formed my reactions to situations and that taking the Alprazolam regularly would leave me better equipped to deal with anxiety. I had set a routine to follow at the beginning of the residency and keeping to this, with regular exercise, writing and meal times, would ensure I'd be tired enough of a night to sleep.

With this positivity of thought I left the cottage to walk the circuit up to the First Basin and back down the zig zag. Rather than take the path leading to the tea rooms, where a leisurely coffee could turn into a laid-back lunch and a loss of resolve, I took the path that led to the river where it narrowed to run between the cliffs, forgetting it was closed because of rising floodwaters. Beyond the barrier, the ford was now a fast flowing rapid with water bouncing over hidden boulders in a dance of freedom. Once, before it had been dammed upstream sixty years before as part of the hydroelectricity scheme, the river had flowed like this in all seasons. Now this was a show only seen when the company increased the cusec release or when the flooded South Esk raised the dam level. With the ford impassable, I'd have to take the longer route over the suspension bridge,

The gravel path was damp underfoot and I detoured in search of a more open route to avoid the run off from drooping branches of the low canopy dripping down my neck, stopping once in a drier area to take a few shots of the rapids through the trees. Even when it wasn't raining, a heavy mist gathered in parts of the gorge, dampening everything in sight. It was part of its charm. I emerged immediately below the tearooms and could almost taste the coffee, one of the best I had tasted anywhere since arriving in Launceston, but determination to stay with the plan kept me strong and I continued on my way. I was pleased I had packed the camera as nature's show presented photographic opportunities wherever I looked, from the rapids below the bridge, where water tumbled as liquid thunder into the swollen basin, to the almost submerged swimming pool rails and the grassed area on the other side, now under threat from the rising water.

This was a vista straight from my childhood, an

excitement of sound and movement that terrified and fascinated, while giving me an odd sense of security that all was well in my world. Strange I'd get the feeling of safety from the chaos of unrestrained floodwaters that roared and eddied in abandon as a metaphor of my life.

There was a cafeteria on this side, built high above the flood marker and just below the chairlift that carried tourists and locals alike, its swooping cables and chairs carrying squealing occupants a travesty to nature in this natural amphitheatre. Added to my distaste was the fact I'd have to walk beneath the drop zone of the cable chairs to reach the beginning of the zigzag, opting instead for the longest route as this offered the best cover from trees and the overhang from the café. This left just a short, uneventful, walk across the grass to where the path began. Why did I always have to worry about things that might never happen? Without the gift of foresight, fate was unavoidable.

A pet hate of mine was the way time and place had so often been sacrificed by the city councillors for trendy money spinners, history overpainted in garish colours and buildings demolished completely to make way for obscenities of modern architecture, grey concrete mausoleums with a limited life span. To some degree I could understand the island's need to mask its dark history of attempted Aboriginal genocide and its convict beginnings, a denial that continued into the twentieth century when no one wanted to own to either convict ancestry or Aboriginality. This changed in the latter decades with people searching furiously for most tenuous link to the unfortunates once so maligned. Convict tourism was now big business, history over-written with an antiseptic wash of gentrification. Gone were the desperate felons of the history I had been taught about in school, replaced one and all with stories of almost genteel poverty and crime by necessity. What remained of the gaols and probation stations had also been given a makeover, a new history preserved behind perspex panels for tourist consumption.

This was almost understandable and didn't compare with the mutilation of the cataract grounds, the skyline forever tainted by the twin cables that carried the cars from the engine house high on the hill to the tearooms on the opposite side of the river. Worse still were the houses built to teeter on the clifftop, as if through liege entitlement, to look down on lesser mortals at leisure. The caretaker's cottage could also fall into this category of vandalism except it had been built for a practical purpose and had been in place long enough to gain its own historical respectability.

Grumbling to myself, I made a concerted effort to keep the ugliness out of my line of sight, taking a few more photos of the flooded basin before, zooming across to the suspension bridge, the rapids and the lush vegetation on the tearoom side. Satisfied there'd be a few good shots amongst them, I left the camera to hang on its strap around my neck and began the steep climb into the scrub. I hadn't meant to use the walk as anything other than meditation and reflection, however, looking down at the river from this height its serpentine form became the opening line of a poem. Persistent in its repetition, like the beginning of so many of my works during their mental formation, I knew I had no need to write the words down this time. They weren't going to be forgotten and I repeated the lines, adding to them as I walked.

There's a place between the basin and the bridge where the dirt path flattens and an old railing allows weary walkers to lean and rest and take in the view, a natural stopping place where the respite lessened the chill of the metal railing. From this position I had a wide-angled view of the north side, where tiny figures of other people braving the cold walked or jogged along the bitumen path and I gained a clearer perspective of the sheer height of the rock face. Using the zoom on my camera as binoculars, I could see dew drops on ferns and the drooping fronds of the sheoaks. Turning to my right, I had a clear sight of the cottage and the cliff rising up to rooftops of the houses on South Esk Road jutting above the highest trees. The view when standing in the backyard of the cottage stopped at the second tier of boulders, with only shrubs and the hint of trees showing above these. Looking at the view from this position put to rest any thought of an intruder entering from the back. Even the most experienced climber would need an axe in one hand during their descent to chop their way through the vegetation. Other features, like a miniature inlet directly below the cottage, were less clear, but would be better defined once I had uploaded the images to the laptop.

The trek from this point was mostly downhill and as I didn't envisage stopping on the home straight I repacked the camera, looking up just as a figure emerged from the area of the steps leading to the cottage and walking the short distance to the tollgate. From there it seemed to disappear into thin air as there was no movement on the bridge and I didn't see anyone pass beyond the toll. I didn't give it too much attention though, as my eyes couldn't be relied upon to record anything accurately over that distance and the figure could just as easily stopped in the alcove at the bottom of the steps to light a cigarette or use their mobile. I was feeling too good to worry about it. So good, that I decided to cross the road for a coffee at Stillwater, a restaurant converted from the old flour mill, before returning home. Although underdressed for this place, I was sure they wouldn't mind at this hour of the day and their coffee was always good. After my earlier abstinence,

I deserved it and the focaccia I ordered with it after hunger pangs reminded me it was well past lunchtime.

Sitting at a table looking out over the river to the yacht club beyond, I added to the poem that had come to me earlier. Engrossed in the words falling onto the page, I was startled when I heard my name spoken, looking around to see Alice standing behind my chair, a bulging folder in her arms.

'Oh, you gave me a fright.'

'Sorry.' She sounded anything but sorry and I wondered at the surliness of this girl, 'I'd hoped to run into you,' she rushed on before I had a chance to ask why, my mouth hanging open with the unasked question, 'why did you tell Zalie what my story was about? It wasn't any of your business what it was about.'

Her voice was raised slightly and I looked around to see if other customers had overheard, grateful I had chosen an outside table.

'Would you like to sit down and talk about it?'

'No, I... all right.' She made a protest out of pulling out a chair and plopping heavily into it. I hadn't picked her for a drama queen when we had first met, but I could see it now and knew the best way to counteract this was to take control of the conversation myself.

'Okay. For a start. Your principal phoned me and asked where your story was,' she opened her mouth to speak but I continued, cutting her off as she'd done to me seconds earlier, 'and yes, she did ask me what the subject had been and while I wasn't about to lie for you or anyone else, I just told her it had been a story, speculative fiction, set in the school,' I held my hand up to silence her as she opened her mouth to speak, 'and I've got no idea what it's all about, not do I want to know,' I was on a roll, 'all I did was accept an invitation to speak at your school, just as I've given talks to many other schools before, without incident, and I think you need to sort out your issues with the person or people concerned.'

This slowed her down, although the anger remained, showing in the cold flash in her eyes and rigid posture. Now she had quietened down, I tried a more conciliatory approach,

'Would you like a drink? A coffee or soft drink?'

'No... thank you.' She added the thank you as an afterthought. Small progress, I thought. 'I just don't see why you had to tell her. Surely you knew I didn't want anyone to know about it when I asked for it back.'

'Well, no, I didn't know why you asked for it to be returned because you didn't tell me and I suggested to Zalie you may have wanted to edit it some more. What I don't understand is why you wrote it and gave it to me in the first place. You're an excellent writer and I'm sure you could have come up with something else.'

'You don't get it do you?'

'Obviously not.'

'You're a writer aren't you? And I wanted to tell you the story, hoping you'd want to write about it. You're supposed to be writing about the cottage aren't you?'

'Well, not just the cottage. I'm writing a novel set in the cataract and general area, which is one of the prerequisites of the residency as determined by the council. There is flexibility however, regarding style, genre, etc.' She nodded her understanding, although I could see the anger remained. Maybe this was a permanent state with her, part of her growing up personality, 'I just can't see what your story has to do with my writing.'

'Didn't you read my story?'

'Of course I did. I made comments on it didn't I?'

'Well?'

I was beginning to think I was in some sort of parallel

universe, with neither of us able to connect with the other.

Alice pushed the folder across the table and expanded on her story, telling me about her mother, Claire, who had been taken for adoption after own mother had given birth to her in the home that now housed the school and how her grandmother couldn't cope with the loss of her child and had suicided some time later. Alice's mother had not fared well with her adoptive family and her dream had been to reunite with the only mother she was prepared to recognise. This had been the one thing that kept her going through the hard times of her childhood and early adult years. It became an obsession that prohibited her from forming meaningful relationships, even with her own daughter, and led to severe mental health issues.

Claire been almost forty when she had Alice and post-natal depression saw her in and out of mental health facilities with Alice eventually placed in foster care. She had been unable to settle into any school until the placement in *The Arches* several years earlier. The informal curriculum suited her need for personal space and when the locked room piqued her interest, she had investigated further. It hadn't taken long for her to establish a link between this place and her mother's story, eventually helping her to access the records that would unravel the mystery of who she was.

Alice had hoped that by helping Claire connect with her own mother, the scars of the past could be healed and they'd have some semblance of family life that had so far been denied her. The reality was far from the happy ending she had envisaged. Once she had handed her mother the information and tools to begin her search, she followed each lead like a person possessed, determined to find the mother of her dreams.

What she found was a death certificate and coroner's

report that detailed events leading up to her suicide. It was scathing in its comments on the running of the home and the forced removal of children from their mothers and placement for adoption, all but placing blame on the people concerned, with recommendations the home be closed.

Claire was mad with grief. She had tried to have those concerned brought to justice for what she viewed as the murder of her mother and the shambles of her own life, petitioning politicians at every level, but no one wanted to listen. In the end she developed psychotic confusion and confronted the religious group who had arranged the adoption, threatening violence and retribution. They called the police and Claire was placed in a psychiatric ward for her own and community protection. Three days later she tricked staff into letting her outside, made her way to the gorge and threw herself off the rocks at the exact spot her own mother had taken her life over half a century before.

It was a sad story, tragic, but it didn't have a place in the novel I was writing.

'It's a very sad story, Alice, although I still don't see why the school would object to it being told.'

'Publicity! What if it did get out that the place is haunted? What do you think that would do to enrolments?' I wished she wouldn't speak with that exasperation in her voice, as if I were an uncooperative child, 'so you see I can't hand in that story. Even if I did they wouldn't publish it.'

'It's just a story.'

'No it's not. It's a true story like I just told you and I've heard the sounds of crying coming from that room and so have other kids. Teachers have heard it, too. Why do you think Zalie's angry with me? It's because she knows it's true and we've all been told not to talk about it, and I suppose that means write about it either.'

'I can't see it's any of my business.' It was getting late and cold now the sun had passed and I wanted to wind this up. I had been sitting much longer than it's polite to do so without reordering and I didn't want to wear out my welcome at the restaurant.

'I just thought you might be interested enough to write about it. My mother wanted people to know and in the end it killed her. I think it's a story that needs to be told because it wasn't just my mother and grandmother. There were hundreds, maybe thousands of people who had their lives ruined because of what happened in that place,' she tapped the folder, 'it's all in here.'

'I'm not sure if I can include it in the book I'm writing, Alice, as I've already developed the outline and written several chapters. Leave it with me to think about and I'll get back to you.'

'The big brush off. People always say they'll get back to me but they never do.'

I could see her vulnerability behind the tough face she showed to the world. I had supposed she was about sixteen or seventeen, mistaking her toughness for confidence, but now all I could see was a lost child.

'I will get back to you, Alice. I always keep my word and I'm happy to make a time to have a look at the information you've gathered,' she looked hopeful as I picked up the folder, 'but I'm not promising anything at this stage, just that I'll have a look and we'll take it from there.'

We made a time to meet at the restaurant the following Thursday and she left as abruptly as she'd arrived.

Claire

I wasn't well and certainly not in my right mind otherwise I'd never have left Alice behind to battle life on her own. And life is a battle, with a new enemy waiting around every corner. Some can be vanquished while others remain resolute, barring entry to wellness and peace. It seemed as if my whole life had been built on a lie with each year building the walls higher until they became unscaleable.

I came here to be with my mother. My real mother, the one society stole from me, not the one who gained ownership through the courts and then used me as her personal property. There's a reason why some women are unable to have children. It's God's way of keeping children safe from the cruel vagaries of the disenchanted. Just as I thought my mother had been waiting for me in life, I expected she'd meet me in death if I entered the water at the same place and I've been looking for her ever since. Sometimes I think I hear her calling my name, or fancy I see her standing against the wall in the kitchen, but as soon as I reach out to her, she's gone. Martha says it won't be long now if only this woman plays her part.

Chapter 11

My head was spinning as I waved apology to the waitress for overstaying and made my way back to the cottage, almost getting skittled as I crossed from one side of the bridge to the other, just catching the words, silly bitch, thrown in my direction, after the horn beeped. I had to agree with them.

When I'd read Alice's story I'd thought it was more fanciful fiction loosely based on fact. Boy, had I been wrong? What a terrible legacy from her mother and grandmother and I could see why she'd want the story told. With the trouble that had come my way from Levi in recent years, when I had no way of stopping him ruining relationships, I wanted someone to hear my story, too. More than that, I wanted someone who could stop him in his tracks, and make sure he received the psychiatric treatment he desperately needed. But there was no one. Even when he broke the law, as he often did, the police weren't interested as he had laid the framework for his delusion with them long before I ever found the courage to speak out. It was my own fault they said, attributing the acts he had committed against me to me. But Alice's story put my own troubles into perspective and I hoped I'd remember this if the night terrors returned.

My mind was so full of what I had just heard, I couldn't get into working on my novel, opting to do some more on the poem I'd begun earlier. The swollen basin brought thoughts of how the river changed with the seasons, and I developed a repetition of the first line to build rhythm and add life to the poem. Satisfied with my progress, I set the poem aside to begin a timeline of the information Alice given me, with one column for facts and another for supposition. I always worked in this way, with the contents of each column interchangeable as information was either proven or disproved.

The history of the home wasn't completely unknown to me. In recent times there'd been numerous reviews and enquiries into a number of past welfare and human service related issues and I wondered if Alice had been involved in any of these, either on her own or one behalf of her mother or grandmother. I suspected she hadn't, hence her frustration with the situation.

While the story didn't fit within my current work, it did interest me and with flexibility in interpretation of this requirement of the residency, I could legitimise time spent on it as working with the community. I had already averaged a workshop per week, with a similar number of group talks and private functions, so assisting a local student with research broadened the experience.

Using *Trove*, it didn't take me long to find information on the maternity home, most of it positive. It had been established at a time in history when support for women, particularly single women with children, was low and infant mortality rates high. Originally intended to provide support and shelter for women and their children, this changed in the early decades of the twentieth century when emerging social standards began to dictate what was acceptable in society, and single mothers and illegitimate children definitely didn't fit comfortably with the suburban landscape and nuclear families.

So many tragic stories.

I filed my findings and the timeline in a new folder for later transfer to Alice and sat back in the silence, letting it carry me into a meditation of just being.

It had been a good day and I expected this air of wellbeing to translate into a good night's sleep, dozing off before I had reached the bottom of the page of the book I was reading, undisturbed when it landed on the floor next to the bed. Positive attitude plays a big part in mental health and I woke feeling rested and refreshed the following day. It was only on waking I realised I hadn't left all lights ablaze as on previous nights. What a difference a day makes.

Then I noticed the book I had dropped on falling asleep had moved. No longer on the floor, it was now on the bedside table with my glasses on top, the bookmark jutting from between the pages. I didn't think much about this until later, when I noticed other things out of place. Not major displacements, as if the place had been done over or ransacked, just a subtle changes of position. My lap top had been closed, when it was always my habit to leave it open except when transporting it. Papers were in tidier piles than I had left them, everywhere I looked something had altered. One Roman blind had been raised a fraction, a glass left on the sink now resting on its rim instead of its base. This is something I would never have done. A country woman had once told me to keep drinking glasses and cups rim side up so mice couldn't make contact with the rim. It made perfect sense to me.

Puzzlement overcame fear on this occasion. How could this have happened?

Had someone entered the cottage while I had been asleep? Or had I walked in my sleep and behaved uncharacteristically?

I didn't allow myself to think of possible paranormal, poltergeist activity. That would be too easy and more likely to lead to another panic attack than the thought of any two legged in the flesh intruder. I checked the locks on doors and windows and could see no sign of entry, forced or otherwise, so I put it down to house movement and got on with my day.

I didn't have time for fanciful thoughts or any time to waste as I had to prepare for an afternoon poetry session. My plan had been to show drafts of poems I had written so far and invite comment on these. It's easier to become bogged down or head off in the wrong direction with any form of writing and I valued the opinions of other poets and writers. I had scheduled some time to discuss the novel, as many poets were writers as well and their view of the direction I had taken was i9mportant to me.

I was also interested in information on the deaths in the river and history of *The Arches* that I could add to Alice's research. My only concern for the day, which I had pushed to the back of my mind, had been the events that followed the last group in the cottage, when the dreams or living had increased, as if opening the door to other nocturnal activities. Still unsure whether these things had really happened, I felt I had pulled myself together enough to deal with any issues should they arise in the future.

The guests arrived in dribbles of twos and threes, more than I had expected and I was pleased to see a mix of gender and age. Often poetry or writing events were mistaken as the territory of retirees seeking to fill their time with hobbies and even more frequently, the domain of women, and this kept many outside this demographic from attending. A surprise for me was to see Jana amongst the attendees and I wondered which hat she'd be wearing for the afternoon, council worker or poet/writer. Like most guests, she carried a clipboard for note taking or in preparation for any writing exercise I might propose, with no sign of the bulky bag she had busied herself with at our first meeting. Another return visitor was Anna, whose home I'd had dinner at some time back. She sometimes stopped in on her way back after her morning jog when we shared a lazy coffee on the balcony. Louise had managed time off from the tearooms to join others I had met at previous events so I felt as if I was in familiar company. My shaky self-confidence left me unsure whether my skill as a facilitator was the attraction or the opportunity to revisit the cottage, but it was all the same to me and all were welcome.

Jana was friendlier than at our first meeting and she apologised for her abruptness on the day.

'You must have thought I was terrible rushing off like that, but I had another place I had to be...' her voice trailed off and I smiled reassurance, because it had been okay, remembering I had been eager to be alone in the cottage.

'It's fine. Don't worry about it. I wanted to settle in anyway. Maybe you'd like to meet up for a coffee and a catch up some time, either here or somewhere that suits you.'

'I'd love that, I really would, and you can tell me how it's going,' she nodded at the full room of people to suggest any private conversation might be difficult, 'how it's really going.' She looked hard at me as she added this.

'It's going good actually. We can make a firm time during the break. It looks like everyone's ready to start now.'

The general hubbub of chatter had quietened, with people looking at me expectantly, so I began on schedule. I liked workshops as a rule, regardless of whether I was an attendee or running it myself. Especially writers' workshops, when a contagious energy lasts long after the session closes and I could feel this vigour building. I broke the attendees into three smaller groups and put three of the poems I'd been working on up for comment, moving between the discussions, listening and adding to their observations. This was followed by informal readings of their own work that had a common subject matter – the Cataract. Written according to preferred style and voice of the individual, all had a quality that showed dedication to the art and I enjoyed the role of listener.

After a short break, I spoke with each participant and commented on their own work. Many poets and writers lack confidence in their own work and sought reassurance when the opportunity arose. I'm talking about retiring poets in this instance, not the more extroverted performance poets who have been gifted with extreme confidence and self-assurance that every word they write and speak has been blessed by the poetry gods. I relate more closely to the shy writer of beautiful verse, those who have no idea of the magic of their words, the true poets as against screamers of words.

We re-formed as a larger group to discuss the progress of my novel. I read short chapter excerpts and invited opinion, taking notes for later reflection, before I opened for questions and the conversation turned to the cottage, as I had expected it would. Most people seemed to have a preoccupation with what it was like to be alone in the cottage after nightfall, almost seeing this as some kind of witching hour. This said a lot to me about the position of the cottage and its isolation, although less than a mile from the centre of the city. Others had tales of their own, some an extension of myth, others about the deaths that had occurred in the area, the drownings and suicides from the cliff.

Anna hadn't contributed to this discussion and it was only then I realized she hadn't really bought into the subject the night of the dinner at her house either. I wondered if she knew more about the cottage than she had said.

Louise remained after the others had left and we shared a bottle of wine on the balcony, rugged up against the cold, watching the traffic build up on the bridges and the dull brown of rushing water below.

'We heard some good poetry today.' Louise was the first to break the silence.

'Wasn't it? I love it when people gather to share their work. Not only because it takes the load of me to deliver, to perform in some way, but I'm genuinely interested in what others create.'

'I've always found the atmosphere of the gorge lends itself to reflection and imagery of words. Some of my favourite poems have been written during slow times at work, when I can take a few minutes to listen and take in the sounds and scents around me and write about them. It's truly a mystical place, hauntingly so at times. Do you find that?'

'I've always felt it, even as a child. Sometimes in an oppressive way, but also a spiritual haunting is probably the best way I can explain it. I suppose it shows itself in different ways to the individual, depending on what's happening in their life.'

'I can see that. There can be a sense of brooding that I imagine adds to the hopelessness felt by those contemplating taking their own life,' she paused, as if reflecting on her own words before continuing, 'there have been so many deaths here since white settlement, ones we know about that is.'

'Yes, I've done a bit of research into the drownings and cliff falls, accidental or otherwise. I don't know, if I was going to end it all I don't think I'd do it here. With my luck I'd botch the job anyway. No, this would be the last place I'd want to die.'

'I'm the same. Not that I spend a lot of time thinking about it. I always think death will tap me on the shoulder soon enough without me chasing it.'

We talked on until the cold chased us inside and she left to walk the short distance to her home, although I didn't envy the walk uphill to South Esk Road. I hadn't realised she was

Anna's neighbour or that her house almost overlooked the cottage until she mentioned it as she was leaving. She could be either spy or guardian depending on how I looked at it. I preferred the latter.

Stella

My battered body travelled some distance from where I went in, coming to rest in the mud at Stephenson's Bend, and mine was a case of murder if ever there was one. My husband was a brutal and ruthless man who had beaten me throughout our marriage. Only those who have lived on the end of a man's fists can know the futility of escape and the loss of motivation that control brings. In the end it became the normality of my life and I put up and shut up until the day he brought his girlfriend into my home. This was the final insult and I told her she had to go and this caused the final, fateful row when he battered me to within an inch of my life before I managed to get out of the house and hide in the back paddock. He found me there and beat me again until I lost consciousness and he tied my hands and put gag over my mouth.

They told so many lies, him and his fancy woman, saying I'd thrown a hammer at his back and tossed boiling water over him as a reason for his beating me. He was good at that. He even told police he'd been down to the river looking for me, covering his tracks in case he'd been seen when he disposed of my body later that night. I lay bleeding in the paddock for hours while he and she sat inside plotting their story and covering their tracks. They even wrote a suicide letter they stuffed in my coat pocket before frogmarching me down the street and over the flats to the river where, with one punch to the head, he rendered me unconscious again before removing the ties and gag and throwing me into the river.

They were so sure of getting away with it they didn't

even report the matter to the police.

People knew the true story, but there was no evidence. The coroner went as far as saying they had driven me to my death, but they were free to carry on their sordid relationship although they were subject to so much vitriol and public condemnation they left the state.

It's peaceful where I am but true peace will only ever come from the telling of the truth, that my husband murdered me and his mistress helped him with an alibi and to dispose of my body. I had hoped this writer at the cottage would be the one to tell my truth, but it seems this isn't the kind of story she writes. Martha tells me she will help my story to be told one way or the other.

Chapter 12

Community activities brought invitations to lunch, dinner, writing groups or coffee that, if I were to accept them all, would leave me no time in which to write. I made a mistake in accepting Anna's invitation the first week and this increased the expectations of others, but I covered that by holding groups at the cottage and attendance at local writing groups, where I explained my position and writing responsibilities without having to repeat this endless times. I had now fulfilled my community obligations, leaving a solid block of writing time until I was to meet Alice in a few days.

Louise helped me tidy up after the guests has left and I was pleasantly surprised to see someone had done the dishes without me even noticing. Women could be like that, carrying their housekeeping instincts as a fall-back position in some social situations. I had done it myself many times when I wanted five minutes away from a crowd, or conversely, when I felt the need to be helpful or included in group activities, being on the end of a tea towel brought a sense of useful belonging and entry into the camaraderie of women.

Some kind soul had even organised the leftovers on a tray for my evening meal. I made a mental note to send a thank you message to all participants. Getting visitors to sign the guest book meant I always had a record of addresses and I looked through the list of names to refresh my memory. Hard to believe there had been twenty-one people packed into the small space and yet it hadn't felt cramped at any time. Having plenty of planned movement in and between activities helped and there was always the overflow into the kitchen and balcony that maximised the space.

Whether because of the flurry of activity throughout the afternoon, the cottage had a restless atmosphere and I couldn't settle at any given task. I persevered for a while but words, when they did come, weren't the ones I wanted and the delete button was in overdrive. This happened sometimes after a workshop, when there'd been no cooling down period before going on to the next activity and after too much caffeine.

I became so used to the pattern of noise from the outside world that I could tell the time without looking at the clock. The steady drone of traffic had eased, although the sound of vehicles was muted by the river in its rush to converge with its twin from the north, swirling the bowl of the Tamar in their excited meeting. If there was any pedestrian traffic on the path or determined joggers, their footsteps were inaudible. Too tired to do any mental work, but too awake to sleep I sat in contemplation of the day, to process the workshop, uneventful though it had been, and the people who had attended. I was thinking about my conversation with Louise when the first words were spoken.

'Why do you keep bringing people here? I've told you it's not your place.' And there was Martha, her face an angry red, glaring at me.

I was awake. I knew I was. So how could this be happening?

I turned the television up and swallowed my fear, but it didn't digest too well, fluttering in my stomach as the woman continued.

'I wanted to be your friend. I really did. I thought you were like me, that you liked the peace and quiet, but then you go and fill the house with noise, even the kitchen isn't safe with its chatting, giggling people,' she looked at me in that calculating look of hers and for a moment her face morphed into Alice's, 'they're not your friends you know and some of them don't think much of your poetry either. Not that I can blame them for that. It's not very good and it doesn't rhyme. Makes no sense to me. I hope your book turns out better.'

I wanted to be conciliatory and ignored her provocations. It was, after all, her house. I was only a temporary resident. A few weeks and I'd be gone.

'I'm sorry, Martha. I prefer to be on my own too, but staying in the cottage means I have certain responsibilities and having people visit from time to time is one of them.'

Even as I was speaking, my mind was elsewhere. I wondered who had made negative comments about my poetry, then just as quickly chastised myself for letting it matter. I never expected everyone to like my style, or even the work I produced, and it usually didn't worry me when they didn't. Bad manners were another matter altogether though and it was poor form to speak about someone in their own home, even if their stay was temporary.

'Well, I hope it doesn't happen too often, that's all I can say. It upsets everyone and I can't settle the children after.'

'The children?'

'I've wanted to speak with you for a while now but if you're not carrying on like a mad woman, you're racing around the countryside until you're that tired you can't hear me when I do speak.' I noticed she had swept right over my question about the children, 'you see, one of the things I really don't like about having you arty types in the cottage is the hangers on that come with you.'

She was off on a tangent and I thought it best to just let her run with it. The sooner I found out what it was she wanted from me, besides a return of peace, the sooner she might leave me alone.

'The thing is, most of them don't even know. They're so out of touch with themselves. They come here, do what they call art, a bit like you trying to write poetry, and they're oblivious to the real stories of the cottage. I thought you were different, that you were interested in the cottage and the women who live here. And I thought I could help you with your problems with Levi.'

I noticed she spoke in the present tense when mentioning the women but it was her mention of Levi that jolted me to respond.

'Levi? What could you know of Levi?'

'I know what he's done to you and what he's still doing to you, except you're too caught up in yourself to see this. More importantly, I know what he's going to do and that's what I could help you with.'

This had to be another trick of Levi's. He was clever, I'd give him that, and smoke and mirrors was right up his alley. On the other hand, I had yet to be convinced he knew where I was or even that I had changed my name. How could he when I had been so careful, taking my time with every part of the process, always looking behind and around me before moving on to the next step.

'Your know what Martha, or whoever you are, if in fact you're even real at all, I think you just like playing games. If you know about Levi, then that must be because you're in league with him. God, you could even be him for all I know.'

'I know about Levi. Take my word for it or ignore it at your peril.'

'But how…?'

'Never you mind. I can fix the Levi problem, but I need you to help me first.'

I felt like that other Alice, that I had fallen down some rabbit hole and this was my own personal Mad Hatter – or

Queen of Hearts.

'How could I help you?'

'I don't feel like talking any more right now. I'm needed in the kitchen,' a child cried as if on cue and I could hear whispers and rustling from the other room and she disappeared as quickly as she had appeared. I could only just make out her last words, 'if you want to know about Levi, have a good look at those pictures you took the other day.'

Well, at least she had left me with something, besides a sense of panic, although I wasn't sure I wanted to know. Would it be helpful to know if he was about or would this add to my fear, and what could I do about it anyway?

I was sure the police in Tasmania wouldn't be any different to their Victorian counterparts and would believe any information given to them from that state. Levi had stitched me up so tight in labelling me as a nutter, I knew I'd never get assistance or justice in that quarter.

I cogitated for a while longer before the urge to know overtook the need for peace and I opened the image editor to the date concerned, surprised at the sheer volume of pictures I had taken in that short while. There were over three hundred images taken at different stages of the walk, but I felt the ones Martha referred to were those taken of the cottage from the opposite side of the gorge.

I remembered the inlet below the cottage I had noticed through the zoom and opened these first, adjusting the enlargement to just short of pixilation. All I could see was a small inlet created by the formation of the rocks, a dark place with the higher level of the river and overhanging branches almost hiding it completely. There was nothing suspicious here that I could see. Maybe when the river was running low a small dinghy could slide in and if, and only if, there was an opening in the rock face, would a person be able to make their way into the foundation space of the cottage. I'd been known to be fanciful in the past, I was a writer after all, but any stretching of the imagination in this instance would serve no useful purpose.

Turning my attention to higher up the cliff face, to the area immediately above and to the side of the cottage I still couldn't see anything out of the ordinary, even on the highest zoom setting. Maybe Martha had been referring to the view of the cottage itself from where the photos and been taken, which gave a panoramic view of the whole area. These images showed inside the windows right down to the placement of furniture in the two living rooms. I could plainly see my laptop open on the desk and with a more powerful zoom lens, or binoculars, I thought with growing discomfort, I could have read the screen quite easily. I imagined Levi squatting in the damp grass, well-practiced in his role of stalker, reading the screen as I typed or information I researched, even watching my reaction to the comments of the blog post.

If this had been what Martha had indicated, I rectified it immediately, moving the small desk to the other side of the room and placing the laptop so I looked out over the river and the cliff face as I worked. First problem solved, the other insurance was in making sure I kept the blinds on that side of the cottage closed at all times, unless I chose to look out. This seemed a sensible thing to do anyway, Levi or no Levi, as you never knew who might be lurking about the place with its fortuitous voyeuristic opportunities. The distinctiveness of the cottage and its unique setting made it one of the most looked at, photographed, and speculated on, sites in the city, for tourists and locals. It followed that artists and writers in residence became something of a curiosity by default. Anytime I was on the balcony or in the side yard when walkers passed below they always called a greeting, some looking expectantly for an invitation to climb the steps. One day, when I had been on my way out, a woman around my age moved across the path to mount the steps as if my presence gave open entry to anyone. She asked me why I was there and if I lived in the cottage, all the while coming closer to the latch gate before I managed to dissuade her from entry. On another occasion the captain of a tourist launch that regularly carried passengers from Home Point to the first cataract, included a run down on the occupancy of the cottage in his talk over the loudspeaker, while those on board waved madly as if I were a visiting celebrity. I didn't mind this so much, as I could always choose to remain inside when the launch passed. I quite liked the anonymous contact as passengers called greeting from a distance, like a line from Longfellow's *Tales of a Wayside Inn* - Ships that pass in the night, and speak each other in passing from...

Only my ship was real and it passed day and night without me seeing it and it had a name – Levi.

I sat down at the desk in its new position and examined the images carefully, magnifying each section by section, looking for the point of a needle in a haystack.

The only thing wrong with the desk in this position was it put the door into the room behind me and I had never been comfortable with that positioning. It came down to fight or flight stress response. In any situation, whether at home or at work, or even sitting in a café or restaurant, if I had the choice, I always positioned my chair to where I could see the door from any angle. If Levi was coming for me as he had threatened on so many occasions, I wanted to at least see him coming. I scanned every detail in the images; one eye squinted in concentration as I searched every possibility.

The blanket of shrubs above the house thinned in parts and I could just make out sections of the path that led from the bridge to the road at the top. I concentrated on this, looking for any anomaly that couldn't be explained as rock or vegetation. I wondered which rooftop belonged to Louise and Anna's houses. They were all huge, stunting the cottage in size as well as position.

My heart skipped a beat when I saw what appeared to be the figure of someone standing, not on the path, but half crouched in the scrub, head bent as if looking down on the cottage. I couldn't make out the size or any distinguishing features that might tell me the age or gender and whoever it was appeared to be wearing a hood of some sort.

Could this be the same person I had seen lurking around the steps the day the shots had been taken?

I had assumed after meeting Alice unexpectedly that it had been her and I wished I had asked her at the time. Alternatively, it could have been any person using the track stopping to pick up something they had dropped.

It could have been anyone and I had to keep telling myself that or risk losing the plot completely.

Doris

My story is simple compared to others. I came from Hobart to Launceston hoping a change of scenery might bring relief to the depressing moods I had experienced, so deep I could not find any joy in life or hope for the future. There was no foul play involved and I left behind a note to make sure my intentions were known. It was like a game of Russian roulette. If the note was found in time and a search party found me I might have been inspired to go on. If not then it would be the long drop off the rocks near the old dam into the river.

The river won.

Depression is an age old malady that needs to be listened to. This river has played host to far too many sad beings who, either by nature or life events, have felt there was no other recourse available to them. My years in the river have given me time to reflect and I implore any person suffering these dark moods to speak to others, tell people what you're feeling and ask for help. If I can save one person with this advice my time in Kama Loka will be over and I can pass on to the next level of soul existence.

Chapter 13

The medication and my recent resolve must have been working otherwise I'd have been a basket case after recent revelations. As it stood, while I was terrified Levi may know my new identity and even be in Launceston, and having had recent interaction with a ghost of some sort who seemed to know my every move, I was somehow holding it together. Marcus would have been proud of me, either that or think I had lost the plot completely.

I had gone as far as I could with the research for Alice and wished I had arranged to meet with her earlier to get it out of the way. It felt like having the material was holding me back from my own writing as I often gave in to the temptation to look further into her claims, knowing as I did so there was nothing else to find in digitised records. She'd need to go to the local library and work her way through microfiche records and contact state government records departments if she hoped to take it further. Ultimately though, I couldn't see any joy for her in her search. I had met people like her before who really had no interest in any findings that didn't support their story. It was tragic her mother and grandmother had died in the manner they had, but all the finger pointing and blame laying wouldn't bring them back, nor would it give her any peace. Sometimes it was better to express unhappiness with a situation, accept what you can't change, and move on.

My online research had brought up various contemporary accounts of the maternity home and accusations against the organisation involved, most of which wouldn't stand the defamation or libel test if brought before a court. The majority of what I read were personal account blog posts about past adoption practice, the more insidious ones written under the name of a network or organisation, but all clearly written by the same person pushing their own agenda of baby selling and corrupt practices. I could see how this might happen when an adult adoptee, unable to accept their own mother had, to use the language of the day, 'given them away', might look for factors that would lessen her involvement. *The Inquiry into Forced Adoption*, primarily driven by birth mothers, focussed on their lack of power in decision making regarding their babies at the time of their birth, however, assertions about that period that relied upon bullying others into a submission of a stated belief left me feeling uncomfortable.

Some of the misinformation, published on the internet as factual, related to the home in Launceston. I could see how damaging and misleading this could be to any person seeking information, either about the home or their biological parentage, presented as it was from so many web sites, albeit by the same misguided person, and how this could be accepted by many as the truth. For Alice, if she believed her mother had been stolen from her own mother and sold to new parents, it would add to the grief she already experienced through her own loss

If she was able to move past her need for a futile apology from those who had nothing to do with what had happened, or had no knowledge of it until it had been brought to their attention via reviews and inquiries, then she had the makings of a great story. Alternatively, if she wanted to use her investigative skills to write an account that could be backed up factually, she'd have an equally good book, but anything full of supposition and assumption, such as some of the rubbish published on the web, would never make it past the slush pile of any publishing company.

Setting the research aside for what I hoped would be the last time, I opened my poetry file. Feedback was always welcome and if someone saw my work as not up to scratch, as Martha suggested, then I needed to look at it through their eyes to see where it could be improved. I had presented it at the workshop in draft form and it was possible the person who made the negative comment hadn't understood that. However, once I had opened the file, I found my concentration lacking, thoughts of Levi consuming any creativity before it had a chance to take hold.

The image of the figure on the top path brought back memories of his previous stalking, when I had lain awake wondering when he'd strike next or which member of my remaining family, the ones he had yet to win over, he would target for attack. From intimidating drive-bys, to turning off utilities in the middle of the night or making nuisance calls to local and government authorities, he was relentless in his persecution, all the while claiming to those he was grooming that he was the victim. While I lived in terror behind locked doors and closed window blinds, he walked freely and unmolested. I had used the last of my reserves in moving beyond his reach and I knew I could go through it again.

Staring into the image of the blurred figure, the questions circled.

Was it tall enough or thick set enough to be Levi or slight enough to be Alice, or had it simply been some person walking the path and stopping for a rest half way up the steep steps?

I tortured myself for some time before taking control of the situation and calling out to Martha, damned if I was going to wait until she was ready to show her face again. If she had information then I wanted to hear it, good or bad. It was probably a sign of my deteriorating mental state that, while I thought I was functioning within the bounds of sanity, I was accepting the existence of Martha without fear or question.

'Martha.' I called her name loudly several times before she answered and I could tell by the tone of her voice that I had caught her off guard. Good.

'What do you want, woman, screaming out like that? You'll wake the whole household up.'

I was about to say sorry, apologetic as always, but stopped myself before giving away my advantage.

'I want to know what you know about Levi, if in fact you do know anything.'

'I know what he's done to your life and your fear that he'll find you here.'

'How would you know any of that?'

'There's a lot that I know, more than I'd like to know sometimes. Other people's secrets find their way to me and I keep them safe until it's time to let them out.'

'I don't understand why you'd have Levi's secrets. He wouldn't share these with anyone, not even himself. That's a big part of the trouble.

'I didn't say it was Levi's secret. It's really your secret isn't it? Your new name and identity. Isn't that a secret?'

This woman was so annoying when she chose to be.

'And someone's been hanging around here while you've been out.'

'Who?'

'Don't know. Fanny told me.'

'Was it the girl, Alice?'

'Alice!' A look of concern crossed her face. 'She's a troubled one, too, just like her mother and grandmother. You need to look out for that one.'

'It's not my place to look out for her. I'm…'

'The responsibility belongs to all of us. It goes with living in the cottage. It's what we do. I've been doing it for over a hundred years and I'm weary of it all, but I can't rest until I find someone to take over.'

'There are others here. I've heard them talking.'

'They're the rescued, not the rescuers, the ones who need taking care of… and their children.

I took up from where she had interrupted me, '…just here for a short while. A visitor.'

'Well you should have thought of that before you came here, shouldn't you? What did you want? All the glory as a writer? To feel important?'

'If you knew as much about me as you claim to then you'd know why I'm really here. And why me? There've been dozens of artists and writers in residence here since the program began so why single me out?'

'Because I couldn't get through the thick skulls of any of them. I tried, God knows, I tried, but I couldn't wake any of them from their earthly intentions. They couldn't hear me. You did. It took a while and I had to go to extreme measures to draw you out,' she wiped her hands on her apron as if to signify the end of one task before moving onto the next,' but you're ready to go now and that's all that matters isn't it?'

She offered one of her rare smiles and the tiredness at the corner of her eyes lifted slightly and, although I was loathe to disillusion her, it was better to nip it in the bud.

'Martha, I'm sorry, but I really can't be any help. Honestly, it's all I can do to help myself these days…'

I told her about the last ten years, how Levi's persecution began over a simple family dispute that he refused to let go of, even after others had made overtures of peace, going to extraordinary lengths to portray himself as a victim while stalking me and grooming others to extract revenge on his behalf. She remained still while I spoke, without her usual interruptions, just nodding wisely and reaching out to pat my arm in sympathy when I told her of the loss of family, as he persuaded them through his lies and manipulations that I didn't care for them, of falsifying police charges and using others contaminated by his hatred to perjure themselves.

'...and this residency was planned as the last step in forging a new identity and a place in the literary world. I'd love to help you, I really would Martha, but I'll be finished here soon and back to the new life I've made for myself in Melbourne.'

'Be that as it may, and I know all you say to be true, as well as many other things he's done that haven't been brought to your attention, you have a role to play here. You help me and you will be well rewarded, I promise you.'

'But I don't see how...'

She cut me off again. 'All you have to do is play your part and not worry about mine. Set the women and children of the house free and convince Alice of the truth, that there never was any conspiracy. It was just the times we lived in, as harsh and unfair as that was. If she follows her mother and grandmother off that cliff there'll be no peace for her in this life or the next. You asked about the other women in the cottage, well they're the ones I couldn't save from their pain. They're the ones who got by me when I was busy looking elsewhere, doomed forever to cry for their children, just as the lost children cry for the mothers they can't see,' she put her head in her hands, 'I'm so tired, so very, very tired. All my loved ones have long gone and I need to be with them,' grabbing my hands she implored, 'please do this Franny. You will have your peace and we'll be set free.'

Hannah

I had been unwell for some time and recently spent time in the public hospital. The problem was no one ever knew exactly what was wrong with me and I felt they didn't take my complaints seriously. It was pain in my heart and high temperatures that left me so debilitated that all I could do was attempt to cool my head with cold compresses. I had been staying with my aunt since my last discharge from the hospital as my mother found it difficult to cope with my illness and I now felt my aunt was also losing patience with me. There were no answers. It seemed the world would be better off without me in it and I obliged.

It was no act of sadness on my part and I was happy and at peace with myself once I had made up my mind, even chatting to the caretaker on the way up the cliff path. My message is one of comfort for those left behind after an altruistic suicide, to know it was the true wishes of the departed and not an act of sadness that may have been prevented by kindness or attention.

Sometimes death is the only choice.

Chapter 14

Once I had struck a deal with Martha, albeit a reluctant one on my part, there were less disturbance of a night and more interaction during the day as one by one the women of the cottage revealed themselves to me, stopping for a chat when I made a coffee or sitting quietly in the easy chair as I worked. They shared their stories with me, and I wrote them down as they requested, so their side of the tale could be told.

There were women who had left their previous lives suddenly and under great duress, at a time when they could see no way out of their predicament or grief, and they felt their actions had been misunderstood and condemned as either acts of lunacy, cowardice or crime. Others had played no part in their death, victims of violence and murder, who wanted nothing more than their killers to be named.

Now the pressure was off in one way, writing became easier, even working on three projects at once, the novel, which had priority, researching and recording answers for Alice ready for our next meeting, and noting names and dates and writing drafts of women's stories. I continued to write poems as they came to me, thinking to publish these as a stand-alone volume at some time in the future.

I begged off invitations I received, citing the urgency to complete my work, seeing only Louise and Anna, who popped in occasionally at the end of her run. One day Anna stopped by with takeaway coffees and we sat on the balcony watching the river, waving as royalty to the passing tourist launch. I was tempted to tell her about Martha and Levi, but guarded against this. Loose lips sink ships they used to say and it still held true. I wasn't about to put the rocky boat of my life on the line and, as I chided myself later, what would be the point in going to the trouble of changing my identity only to blurt the story out to an almost total stranger. Instead I asked her about the path leading to her street that went past the back of the cottage and the volume of pedestrian traffic it attracted, telling her how difficult I found the trek the day I walked up to Trevallyn. I hadn't realized the night I went to her house for dinner exactly where she lived as I'd taken a taxi that had to follow the road with all its bends and turnoffs. All I had known was that it overlooked the city and mountains beyond with a magnificent view down the river.

'By the time I was half way up I was about done in. Like the grand old Duke of York, I was neither up nor down so I felt I had to keep going. It was only a few of days after I'd hurt my knee and I probably shouldn't have tried it.'

'I hadn't realised you'd had an accident.'

'Oh, it wasn't anything much, I bumped into a cupboard in the dark and it swelled up a bit. I rested it for a day or so and then thought exercise would be the best.'

'And was it?'

'Not at the time, but in the long run, yes.'

We talked about my novel and I showed her my latest poems, watching her face for any tell-tale sign that she may have been the one Martha had overheard talking in the kitchen, throwing out an invitation to comment further.

'I suppose they're not everyone's cup of tea. I think there were a couple of people at the workshop who were disappointed in what I presented.'

'Oh, do you think so?' She looked surprised, maybe not at what I said but because I had even mentioned it, raising one eyebrow querulously.

Reading the cue and not wanting her to think I was being critical of the group in any way, I fluffed it off. 'I thought some people may not have understood the poems were only drafts,' then, to change the subject, 'I really enjoyed the readings. I always like to hear what others write, don't you?'

'Yes, I do, and I appreciate the opportunity to read my own poetry, too. It's good to get feedback.'

I was happy to have avoided possible insult, even though none had been intended. I had lived in enough small towns to know how things worked. Small places were like families, they could speak how they liked about each other but let an outsider voice honest, if unsuspecting opinion, and the big freeze could set in very quickly. I was just as pleased I hadn't given in to the temptation to tell her about the women of the cataract or the issues with Alice because, while I appreciated local knowledge and input, I had no way of knowing the intricacies of existing social networks and who was related to whom and what reactions might be.

Remembering the way of small towns made it easier to understand the women of the cottage and attitudes that may have driven them to extreme action. It also led me to wonder what the response would be to having their stories written and out there for the world to see. Skeletons in closets are a strange phenomenon, where the majority were keen to open the closets of others while keeping their own firmly sealed against leakage. This was something I'd need to discuss with the women, as I was pretty sure they wanted me to submit them to the local papers as a series of articles.

I didn't know whether the newspaper would be interested or not, but I also didn't want to be at the mercy of a modern day lynch mob so I would suggest holding back on publication until after I had left the state. My intention had been to ask my publisher to use the stories as a compendium to my novel. I wasn't sure this would satisfy the women, or if Martha would even accept this as fulfilling my part of the agreement, but I had to look after my own interests in this as well.

It had been raining all night off and on and I didn't expect Anna to be out running in the wet when she arrived at the front door, a bedraggled, shivering figure.

'What were you thinking, running out in this weather?'

'I'm an idiot, I suppose. I left home during a lull in the rain and got caught. Do you mind if I shelter for a bit before tackling those damned steps?'

I gave her a towel to dry off while I made hot drinks for us both, the rain spattering against the window showing no signs of abating.

'I think it's set in now, but I have to get home and get ready for an appointment after lunch.'

'You can't go back out in this. Look it's sleeting now and it'll be freezing.'

'No choice I'm afraid.'

She got up to leave, folding the damp towel over a chair back and pulling her windcheater out from her body as if to create a pocket of warmth.

'Well, let me lend you a coat then,' I had my old rubberised cape coat with a hood that I'd had since forever and, despite teasing from others, I kept it as I'd never found anything as effective in keeping the weather out, wind as well as rain, 'I have to go out tomorrow morning, so if you could drop it off before then that would be good because I reckon this rain is going to hang around for a while.'

'Sure thing. And thank you. What a beauty this is, she pulled out the coat in emphasis, 'I've never seen anything like it in years. I had one once and regretted not keeping it. That's fashion, I suppose.'

She stepped outside into a hail of icy spears and I was pleased I'd be staying in this day.

'Mind how you go on those steps now. They're bound to be slippery.' My voice floated back to me and I wasn't sure if she had heard until she turned to reply, her face set well back inside the generous hood.

'I'll take it easy. Good job I know them like the back of my hand. I know every inch of those steps, every crag of every rock. If I didn't, I'd take the long way round as wet as it is.'

She waved her fingers through the arm slot in the cape and we both laughed as she left, a hunched figure against the elements.

After pulling out the folder Alice had given to me and printing the timeline file from the laptop, I opened the *Trove* web page, typed *Stony Rise Maternity Home*, and every variation of this I could think of into the search bar, scouring every article or mention or even a remote reference to the place or those connected with it. I had pretty much exhausted it in previous searches, but experience had taught me any variation could bring results no matter how obscure.

Stony Rise maternity home had operated between the late 1800s and 1960s. The function of the home had been, to a greater degree, driven by the social change and attitudes that influenced policy and practices, which had led to an increase in separation of mothers and their children through adoption.

I could see much of Alice's research had been undertaken from a position of anger or a need to assign liability, attaching to contemporary blame finding and retributive campaigns that fed her rage and discontentment. Such biased research could only lead to further disillusionment when the answers she sought were not forthcoming. From what I read, it appeared there was a minority of Australian adoptees who did not respect the values and opinions of others, formed through the diversity of the adoptee experience. These people used intimidation to promulgate their expert opinion, an expertise gained through obsessive self-promotion that over-rode or silenced individual voices, denying other adoptees right to hold their personal truth, free of coercion. The greatest revelation for me was in understanding adoption, no matter which side of the triangle a person stood on, equated to pain. It had to be, as it there always had to be winners and losers and this placement was fluid.

Finding impartial, factual and verifiable information requires a painstaking exploration of the data, facts and figures. Unfortunately, Alice had copied material from dubious internet sites in an effort to match her beliefs with attestable evidence. Mixed in with this, was information she gleaned from old newspaper articles about the home and letters from politicians of that era, all then dissected and interpreted to match the propaganda that was feeding her unhappiness.

One blog post I read had been copied and pasted onto dozens of other sites, even those purporting to be acting on behalf of Australian adoptees, which related to the age limits for adoptive parents under the *Tasmanian Adoption of Children Act 1920*. Alice had quoted this to me as evidence of illegal practice and trafficking of babies during the time of her mother's adoption. Closer examination showed that, whereas the Registrar General had set age guidelines in response to the increased demands for children for adoption, these were guidelines only. They had not been legislated as required practice, therefore were not compulsory under law.

Applicants outside of the age guidelines could still apply to adopt, with each judged according to their individual circumstances. I could find no information giving the reasons for granting an adoption outside the recommended age guidelines as it appears these had not been recorded on a case by case basis. I was sure Alice, young though she was, would be able to see how this had led to the speculation by those with an axe to grind about past adoption practices in Tasmania, although it required a huge stretch of the imagination to assume money had changed hands.

Results from the internet search results had been an exercise in walking in the shadow of another such as Levi. I had learnt enough about personality disorders in recent years to recognise it when I saw it. I couldn't blame Alice for the beliefs she had developed, for this was grooming on a mass scale. If Levi had been the battering ram of personal opinion, this writer of this stuff, Graeme Rogel, was the absolute wrecking ball and, whereas Levi had kept his grooming targets low in numbers by comparison, this Graeme had influenced tens of thousands through his manic internet activity. His theories, although poorly researched and written, had been posted and shared on websites claiming expertise on the subject of adoption, most of these sites being of his own creation, such as *Australian Adoptees Authority*.

He shared his findings with government and nongovernment bodies, never missed an opportunity to attend any adoption related activity, review or apology in every state, and gave media interviews at almost the same frequency as the Kardashians. He wrote to politicians and people of influence as the spokesperson for Australian adoptees until his propaganda had been accepted, in many quarters, as truth. A dangerous individual, he effectively shut down any meaningful debate initiated by others who questioned his findings with hate messages and reiteration of his own victim status. It would always be the most vulnerable who became drawn in by his distortions of the truth.

I googled his full name and, once I had waded past all the adoptee related sites he had either created or commented on with authority, adoption research pages and other matters, the links to his social media accounts appeared. I wasn't into stalking, having spent so much time being pursued in this manner myself, but I was interested to see if I could find any further compelling evidence of his professed 'truth' for Alice to read it for herself.

I had already read much of his blog, from which I was sure she had obtained most of her information, and his Twitter account, which consisted mostly of links back to his propaganda pages, before clicking on his Facebook page.

This was interesting.

This guy wasn't only an expert on all things related to adoption, past and present, it appears he was an authority on every subject you could think of, from all branches of politics to all denominations of religion. Other than that he was just your everyday racist, bigot, overbearing misogynist who had no time for any opinion other than his own. This was gold. No intelligent person could read his posts, comments, or his responses to comments from others, without realising he was an absolute and first class loony.

Alice had also given me a link to an old newspaper article about the demand for babies for adoption, using emotive language like, 'child hungry couples', who supposedly besieged the *Registrar General in Tasmania* with adoption applications, with the highest demand for female babies. There was mention of the confidential enquiries into the suitability of proposed adoptive parents, looking at the parental age limit, with the child's welfare the paramount consideration. The age limit for people wishing to adopt children from birth had been fixed at forty-five years for women and fifty years for men, however, as I had already discovered, these were guidelines only and not legislated.

Factors relating to the increase in the number of children available for adoption during the thirteen years from pre-World War II 1934 to post-war 1947, were a combination of conservative social attitudes and the baby boom that led to more babies available for adoption. I could find nothing to suggest any conspiracy to deprive mothers of their children for financial gain or otherwise, although I could find plenty of arguments to refute this, which I added to the growing file.

I might not be able to influence Alice from the deceptions she had brought into, but I could at least show evidence that I had taken her claims serious enough to investigate them. Graeme, like Levi, was a narcissist who used gaslighting as a form of manipulation to create an extreme sense of anxiety and confusion in vulnerable people, such as this in the adoption network, to the point where they no longer trusted their own memory, perception or judgment, accepting his versions of events and distorted findings as their own.

Marie

I was on an outing with my school, Sacred Heart College, enjoying a day at the cliff grounds when my accident happened. The sisters had warned us about the dangers of going too close to the rocks, but Winnie and I went with some other girls to look at the water. I saw a fish swimming and stepped onto a rock to get a better view when my foot slipped and in I went. The water was running fast in this place and the current was too strong for me to swim against.

I have only myself to blame and I carry guilt for the grief caused to my loving family. It is this guilt that holds me to this place and I can only leave through the blessing of Our Lady. If someone was to go to the Church of the Apostles and ask The Blessed Virgin to intercede on my behalf I know I could finally take my place with my family who still wait for me.

Chapter 15

Alice was already waiting when I arrived at Stillwater, empty notepad in front of her and pen caught between her teeth as she stared off into space, not noticing me until I sat down opposite her. Her greeting was friendlier than the last time we met and I took that as a positive omen.

Anna hadn't returned my coat as promised and I'd had to wear my old duffle. Good value against the wind, less so against rain, as it had long ago given up its waterproofing and I'd never had it re-proofed, so I was a bit soggy around the edges when I arrived. I was pleased we had chosen a time to meet after the lunch crowd had left, as we'd have to sit inside. Rivulets of rain ran from the ribs of the closed market umbrellas outside, designed to provide shade in the summer more than any wet weather protection. A chill wind blew in from the river, the kind that takes loose clothing, even the closest fitting, and uses this to flagellate any unlucky enough to be braving the elements.

Inside, the slow burning logs in the grate created an ambience of cosy warmth, a mellowness it was easy to slip into after I had taken off my wet coat and hung it to dry on a coat rack provided.

'I've found a few more articles,' Alice flicked papers from beneath her writing pad in a magician's quick shuffle, 'you'll see I'm right about that place.'

She pushed them across the table and I placed them in front of the paperwork I had brought with me, not sure where they belonged in the chronology of the information it already contained.

'I've been busy, too.'

'But did you get anywhere? That's the question.'

'It's difficult to really know where to go without looking at the bigger picture and that's what I've done, using the information you'd given me as a starting point.'

She looked pleased by this statement. I hoped she'd feel the same way when I had finished.

'I've put the information into separate categories. Anecdotal information, where it can be matched with old newspaper reports, with it all noted on this timeline,' I handed her the first sheet, 'this pile here,' I nodded toward the main file, 'holds most of the internet findings, and this lot,' I pointed in the direction of the last lot of papers, 'are to be treated with caution because, while they appear to come from different sources, they've been created by the same person and most of the allegations he makes not only can't be proven, most can actually be refuted.'

She picked up the timeline, eyes darting up and down the page and across the entries, stopping at her grandmother's and mother's names and running her finger across the page to see what I had written in the spaces. I glanced over the new information she had brought with her, a repetition of what we already had. A different web page identifier, but with the same old hoopla thrown out for the susceptible to grab hold of in their desperate quest for answers. This Graeme, whoever he was, had a lot to answer for, although I suspected he'd never be able to see this.

'Would you like me to go over these with you?' I indicated the third lot of papers.

'Okay.'

That was all she said. Just, okay. As if she didn't care either way. I imagined not showing emotion or enthusiasm was a habit she had developed from a need to self-protect. You couldn't be disappointed if you had no expectations.

When I didn't continue immediately she looked at me, as if trying to figure out what I wanted from her. She plucked at the sleeves of her jacket with nervous fingers, nails bitten and ragged, a symbol of her life. 'I don't know. You seem to be better organised than I am so it's probably as good a place as any to begin.'

'You may not like what I've found and you may not agree with the findings, however, you asked me to see what I could find and this is it,' I smiled to soften the words that had come out sounding harsher than intended, 'all of this information, although appearing to come from many sources, is really the work of one person, Graeme Rogel. He has inundated the internet with his beliefs, which he claims to have extensively researched and validated, to satisfy some need of his own,' I ignored the frown forming on her face, 'and when I examined the copies of letters he presents to support his claims they do the exact opposite.'

'But I met him in Hobart at the *Tasmania Forced Adoption Apology* and I know he's telling the truth. He told me people try to discredit him all the time because they don't want the truth to get out about the home and how babies were sold illegally to adoptive parents.'

'I can't say that didn't happen, although I suspect if it had then he wouldn't be trying to rewrite history to fit his need to believe it happened that way. I can see there was a loophole in the law that did allow for a premium to be paid, but there is absolutely no evidence, not one single whisper that this ever occurred.'

'What about the copies of letters he has?'

'I've read them all and gone over them with a fine tooth comb. In the end they're only letters that speak of possibilities, not facts.'

'What about that person who represented the religious organisation that ran the home at the inquiry, who lied and said they'd never had a home in Launceston?'

'Yes, I've read the rants Rogel has made concerning this. I've also read common sense responses from other adoptees stating that he has either twisted or ignored huge swathes of their words in abusive response. I'm sorry, Alice, the man is quite unbalanced and a menace to any person in the adoption community seeking to learn the truth or to find their own acceptance of what occurred so long ago.'

'He's also emailed me heaps of times and warned me people would speak against him.'

'I don't speak against him, but when I'm asked to do something, such as you asking for help with this, I make sure I do it properly. If I can't verify information from three separate sources then I never include it in my findings. If you want to be a writer one day, particularly in the nonfiction genre, this is a good rule to remember because it may save you from libel and defamation charges.'

'How can he write it if it's not true?'

'I suspect this is because no one's ever taken legal action against him, probably from a position of compassion, because it's not too hard to see he's not well, psychologically that is.'

'I still don't see how it's not true. It's all over the internet, even on sites like *Australian Adoption Authority* and why would they publish information that isn't true?'

'Because he is the administrator of *Australian Adoption Authority* and many other groups claiming to speak for adoptees, as well as those on social media that present as Australia-wide organisations established by adoptees for adoptees to provide mutual support and understanding and act as lobby groups for adoptees rights and services. Take a look at some of the links I've given you and you'll see what I mean. This one here for instance,' I tapped the tip of my pen against a blue link address, 'has no posts made by anyone except him, always under the name of the community, and you'll see there have been no comments made by anyone else on the page. It's just one of the dozens of methods he uses to promote his own beliefs and turn this into other people's truth.'

'That's just not possible. Who would have enough time to do this?'

'A person who's never been able to accept his mother gave him away, regardless of whether she felt she had a choice or not, and who has recreated her as a victim in order to claim victimhood for himself.'

'Do you really think so?'

'Well, I'm no psychologist, but it is my considered opinion.'

'But he seems like a nice man.'

'I'm sure he is and probably well meaning, however, that doesn't make what he's doing right. There's a lot of vulnerable people in the adoptee community, those who have been denied answers all of their life, like your mother, who will naturally gravitate toward someone claiming to have those answers, particularly when they appear to be made from a position of authority.'

'Mmm, I'll need to think on this for a while. It's not that I don't believe you. It's just that I have met him and he's always replied to my emails...'

'That's okay. You need to do what you feel is right for you. I could hardly be pointing out his shortcomings when it comes to exerting influence on others and then do the same thing myself, could I?'

I changed the subject to her writing and the story I had

read and she filled me in on what had transpired at school, how Zalie had quizzed her for a while about the story she'd taken back before accepting a poem she had written in its place.

The conversation then drifted to general matters while we waited for a coffee refill. I stopped myself from querying whether someone her age should be drinking coffee at all, chiding myself to step into this century. The Alice who talked about her interests and likes and dislikes was a lot more likable than the Alice weighed down by the chip on her shoulder. She asked about the work I had been doing at the cottage and I told her about the novel. I also mentioned the women of the cataract, suggesting the idea had come from my research into the cottage and the area. I was at a loss to explain the manifestation of Martha to myself, so I could hardly explain it to someone else. I told her I was thinking about writing a series of stories once the main work had been completed. This struck a chord with her inner writer and, when she engaged immediately with the idea, I invited her to the cottage the following week for lunch and to look at some of the drafts of the women's stories I had already compiled. I was about to ask if she needed permission from her foster carers or even the school before accepting my invitation, but the independent action she had shown so far told me it wouldn't make any difference if she set her mind to doing something and I didn't want to lose the ground I had already made in the last hour or so.

Jane

They said I was a drunk and it could be they were right. It's easy to judge a person for their habits when not walking in their footsteps. Yes, I drank, whenever I had sixpence to buy a draught or two. I drank because I'd been weaned on a gin soaked rag, because it warmed my belly in the old country winters when pickings were slow, and in Newgate Prison where I pandered to the old lags. I drank to blot the memory of the place of my birth, for the children lost to the river because I had no way to care for them, and to escape the pointing fingers and mocking laughter from those who knew no better. I drank to escape the misery of the Invalid Depot until I slipped and fell in the water. God's just punishment for my wickedness I suppose, to leave me in the drink until my lesson had been learnt. Like transportation with a life sentence, it's purgatory without end unless someone can hear my sad tale and offer me a hand up to heaven.

Chapter 16

A surprise phone call from Jana decided my activities for the day when she invited me to meet her for lunch. We hadn't had the best start the first time we met, although we got along fine the day of the cottage workshop. After arranging to meet at a café close to the library, I set out early to allow time to spend time in the research section of the library. I still hadn't seen Anna and wondered if she had knocked on the door while I'd been in the shower. I didn't know her that well, but I had taken her at her word when she said she'd return my coat the following day. Still, I knew better than many how life had a habit of getting in the way of good intentions so I didn't worry too much. If I hadn't heard from her by the following morning I'd chase her up to see if all was well.

It was another bleak day, overcast in characteristic Launceston winter fashion, although the rain had slowed enough for me to walk the few blocks into town. Beneath King's Bridge the muddy brown water swirled well above the usual tide mark and I walked, head down against the wind, avoiding puddles on the footpath to keep my feet dry as long as possible. I hated wet feet, a reminder of school days when the smell of damp woollen socks and leather shoes permeated the winter classroom, a miasma that reduced breath to hard earned pants.

I had placed my papers in a clip down waterproof satchel. No point in having soggy paperwork as well as feet. Jana already had an update on my activities through her attendance at the workshop so I'd brought the information on the women of the cottage, which I intended to expand on. I was hoping she'd be interested enough to support my proposal to council to publish the finished work or to endorse it with a recommendation to a mainstream publishing company and perhaps have a councillor write the foreword. I also hoped they'd see merit in this secondary work as an important social history of that era.

The warmth inside the library belied the weather outside and I quickly shed my coat before it became a sauna, holding in the heat in discomfort. Upstairs in the reference section I introduced myself to the woman behind the counter, Della written in friendly long hand on her name tag, explaining my position as writer in residence and the purpose of my visit that day. She couldn't have been more helpful, leading me to a table with ample space to lay out my papers and offering any help required. I hung my coat over the back of the chair, ignoring the damp wool smell it gave off, and got down to business. Using the same timeline I had used for Alice, I tracked the gaps I hoped to fill, writing notes to follow up and highlighting areas where Della might be able to assist.

It was pleasant working in the well-lit room. I wished I had thought of it before. Writing in cafes had the benefit of coffee on tap, but there was also the chatter of other customers, the scraping of chairs and clatter from the kitchen. Here, in the quietness, time passed rapidly and I was surprised when I lifted my head to stretch my neck muscles to see it was almost time to meet Jana.

Outside, the wind had increased, sending what few pedestrians were about scuttling head down between errands. This seemed to be the unique walking stance of Launcestonians in the winter and I mused over the long term effect on their posture, deciding the only way of knowing would be to visit during a warmer season to see if, like sunflowers, they then stood upright with faces turned to the sun. For the moment though, I blended in, walking like a native as I followed the scent of food wafting from the cafe.

The down side of walking at a fast pace with my head down came to me in a thud, when I collided with someone coming from the opposite direction at equal speed. I had yet to detect the radar required to walk safely in this manner. I offered a reflexive apology but by the time I'd lifted my head the other person had gone, as if I had simply bounced off them and they hadn't even been aware of the contact. Turning around and squinting through wind flicked hair I only caught a glimpse before he turned the next corner. But that had been enough to know it was either Levi or his doppelganger I'd seen on the news the night of the panic attack.

I was entering the café before the impact of this new sighting registered and I began to shake as my stomach tied itself into those familiar knots of anxiety. I fought desperately to bring this under control, knowing what the consequences would be if I didn't, looking around for a toilet in case the self-talk babble didn't get through.

'Francesca, over here,' this was just the diversion I needed to take my mind off the urgency, 'I've saved a table for us.'

Jana was waving from across the room. A fortuitous god had placed her at a table next to the green toilet sign and I could feel my stomach contractions ease as I walked toward her, over-enthusing my greeting as I sat down. Sometimes reassurance was all that was required.

'You're shivering, you poor thing. Are you really that cold?'

'It was so warm inside the library I think I felt it more when I stepped out into the wind.' I stood up to take off my coat, but she stopped me before I managed to get one arm out of the sleeve.

'Leave it on until you warm up. This café isn't always the warmest at this time of day, with the door opening and closing all the time. Wait until you've had a hot drink and get rid of those shakes.'

I didn't forget the encounter with the Levi look-alike, but I was able to push it to the back of my mind while we talked about my activities in the cottage and how this might be progressed to the next level. Jana, while pleasant enough, expressed concern that I had deviated from the original project for which the residency had been approved. I updated her on the progress of the novel, offering chapter outlines to demonstrate the plot direction. She glanced over the pages without reading any of it, giving the impression she thought I had neglected the novel in favour of my other activities. I understood this bureaucratic point of view. It was what happened when the wrong skill set was placed in a no fit position. There'd be no help from this quarter in getting the women of the cataract stories published or endorsed. The only benefit to her somewhat negative stance had been it had taken my mind off Levi, while strengthening my resolve to continue working on the additional work. With this thought in mind I returned to the library research section.

Sarah

I went with my friends to hear the band playing at *The Willows*, near the Cataract Bridge and slipped off the rocks into the water. I couldn't swim and when I went under for the third time I stayed down. I was the only child my poor widowed mother had left and I want to tell her how sorry I am for causing her grief. It's always cold down here by the river and I'd like to feel the warmth of the sun on my face or toast my toes by the fire, but I can never get past all those women and crying babies to feel the heat.

If I could find my way out of here I know Mother will be waiting on the other side.

Chapter 17

I was wary as I left the library, on the lookout for Levi or his double and, despite the wind that was blowing even harder than earlier in the day, I kept my head up looking around as I walked. The Alprazolam I'd taken at lunchtime, under the pretence of taking a paracetamol tablet for a headache, had taken the edge of the panic attack that had threatened earlier. It didn't lessen the fear but it did keep it at bay enough for more rational thoughts to take over. The truth was, I didn't really know if it had been Levi or not. There were plenty of men around of a similar build and I had only seen his back as he disappeared around the corner. Post-Traumatic Stress Disorder was like that. It rose up at the strangest times to contort thoughts and confuse visuals, resulting in unpleasant physical reactions that I hated. I hated it also that Levi had visited this fear upon me.

I trudged through the windy streets, seeking shelter from the rain on the lee side where I could, until I reached the boardwalk leading to the bridge, where there was no respite from the weather to be found.

The squall grew with intensity along the river front, stirring the water to a frenzy of high stepping waves. I could see we were in for a dirty night and I quickened my pace to reach higher and warmer ground, wishing once again I had my old mac. Although the duffle coat was made of wool it wasn't as wind proof as the mac and I hoped Anna returned it soon. I should have lent her the duffle but at the time I had thought the mac would give her extra protection, I'd even pulled the flap over to the side of her neck and buttoned it up for her after she'd slipped the hood over her head. This was difficult to accomplish when wearing it, as the hands had to pass through the side slits and the weight of the cape tended to drag the arms back down. It was much easier to have someone do it for you if possible.

The wind caught the latch gate and slammed it shut almost before I managed to get on the other side. At the same time an errant plastic bag blew across the yard and up into the scrub of the rock face and I followed its progress, forgetting for the moment my need to reach the warmth of the house. Like watching birds or kites, the motion of flight is always mesmerising. The bag disappeared into the mist covering the top of the cliff before something else caught my eye, a patch of red hanging between the branches. It had a distinctive colour I recognised immediately.

My coat.

Anna must have left it in the alcove near the front door where the wind had caught it and carried it upward, like the plastic bag. It had caught by the hood on an overhanging branch to sway like a crimson spectre in mid -aunting.

I tucked my bag inside the porch, trusting its safety while I retrieved the mac, then hurried back down to the path and up the steps. Whether from weariness or older age, it seemed that no matter how many steps I took, the coat, like a mirage, always remained a distance ahead, until I was near the halfway mark when suddenly it seemed to be further back down the path behind me. I put this down to the winding terrain and stopped at the lookout spot to regain my breath, looking around for a long stick to use as a grappling hook. Unable to find anything suitable on the ground, I snapped a low lying branch and stripped the sparse leaves and twigs from it, leaving the strongest shoots near one end to use as a vee-shaped hook.

Looking down I noticed slide marks in the clay where someone must have come a recent cropper, noting the railing now bent out over the drop where they'd grabbed it to save themselves. No stranger to slips and falls myself, they had my sympathy. I suspected they'd seen the coat, and how could anyone miss it standing out red against the green and grey of its surrounds, and tried to retrieve it.

Taking care not to tread in their slide, I tested the vertical rail for strength, finding it firmly embedded in its concrete base. Using this to support myself I swung out with the stick extended, holding tight to the rail, swishing the air and missing the target every time. A couple of times I came close, even causing enough draft to create a swaying movement, before other branches twanged back into place as a barrier.

It was beginning to get dark and although I wasn't far from the cottage I wanted to be inside before night fell. I was still wondering how to retrieve the coat or whether to abandon the rescue until the following day when I managed to hook the hem of the coat, lifting it slowly up and toward me. It snagged and as I pushed the undergrowth aside to release the resistance and I reeled back in horror.

Hanging down below the coat, swinging woodenly from my efforts to dislodge it, I saw the legs.

Navy track pants and white joggers.

And then I knew.

The police cordoned off the area and began the long task of forensic investigation and body retrieval. Not that I was watching, I left that up to the ghouls who ignored the weather to stand and point and gawk at the proceedings, while I gave my first informal statement to the police. As the person who had called it in, I became the primary witness unless someone else came forward with more information.

The police surmised that Anna had walked up the steps, stopping at the lookout point where there was a widening of the steps and a railing for those needing extra help to go further. The rock path was slippery where the top soil had washed away by rivulets that coursed down from the hill above to expose the clay underbase. They concluded Anna had leant against the railing, which had bent outward causing her to topple over. A branch hooked the hood of the coat, halting her fall so abruptly her neck had broken.

Although difficult to judge in the cold weather and before a thorough examination had been undertaken, it was believed she'd been there for two nights.

I shuddered at the thought of her hanging there while I had been tucked up in the warm cottage and I blamed myself for making such a big deal of doing the coat up for her. If it had been open maybe it would have slipped over her face when the branch caught it and she could have dropped out of it. Even as I had these thoughts, common sense told me if that had occurred she would have been unlikely to survive a fall from that height, banging off rocks onto the paved area of the cottage yard.

Only if she'd fallen head first, an inner voice tormented, and the circle of self-blame began again.

The only way to retrieve the body had been from the backyard of the cottage but there was no access for a cherry picker and the fire brigade were called to use extension ladders to reach Anna and bring her down, high voltage spotlights lighting the whole area from river to misted hilltop.

The police eventually left, saying they'd need me to come to the station the next day to make a formal statement, the gawkers and the television and newshounds left and it was as if nothing had ever happened, except for the empty coat hook that stared accusingly each time I looked in that direction. While I hadn't known Anna for long or that well, I mourned her passing.

It was hard to take in. She had known that path so well, had walked it in all weathers, even jogged up and down it and I was puzzled as to why she'd stop in the middle of a downpour when she was in such a hurry to reach home and get ready for her appointment. She had no reason to stop that I could think of and I couldn't imagine her having a leisurely rest against the railing and if it had been loose, even slightly, she would have known about it. Living on the edge of the track she had become something of its caretaker by default, reporting damage caused by the elements or natural wear and tear.

Sleep wasn't going to come easily that night and work was out of the question with the turmoil of thoughts chasing around inside my head. I wished I had company and I was beginning to really dislike the cottage, an irrational blaming that comes when events can't be explained. My life had been out of kilter long before I ever came here, however the residency hadn't been the peaceful writing place of my imagination, occupied as it had been with all manner of relics from the past.

I wondered, not for the first time, whether other artists and writers had similar unsettling experiences during their tenure. I had read works and reports left behind in the cottage and on the council website where individuals had written of their experience, but hadn't seen any suggestion of visitations or discomfort. Thinking another read might turn something up, I headed across the room to the bookcase and the large folder that held the records.

It seemed that all past residents had enjoyed their stay and wanted to return, with only one brief mention of the isolation. No mention of night noises of any kind. I was beginning to think it had all been in my imagination, part of a bad dream that followed me into the day, when I noticed something in the folder I hadn't seen before. Designed in the style of an old fashioned obituary card with a heavy black border, it bore a cryptic comment in copperplate print.

LIFE HURTS A LOT MORE THAN DEATH

R.I P.

That what it.

No signature.

Placed in a plastic sleeve, I could have missed it before due to its size, all other pages being regular A4, but the stand out black would have drawn my attention.

'You found it then?'

Martha appeared in that soundless way she had and I wondered how long she had been watching, or if she ever stopped watching at all, a twenty-four hours a day vigilance. More importantly, I wondered how much she knew of the past forty-eight hours.

'You mean this?' I held up the card. 'Why would I need to find it?'

'And why won't you take me seriously?' That was Martha, always answering a question with another. 'Another woman has died and you could have stopped it.'

That hit below the belt, reinforcing the feelings of guilt I already had.

'How could I have stopped it when I didn't know it was going to happen? It was a freak accident. She slipped off the path and the hood of the coat caught.'

'Your coat.'

'Yes, my coat. The coat I lent her out of kindness for her situation when she needed to get home in the pouring rain.'

'And you think it was an accident do you? That someone who knew that path better than anyone just happened to lean on the railing and slip over the edge?'

'The police said...'

'Yes, we all know how clever they are don't we? Like they've never got it wrong before.'

'I did wonder about that, but who would want to kill her?'

'Why do you think anyone wanted to kill her?' She was talking in riddles, going around in circles, playing with me, watching my face intently as she spoke.

'It was him, wasn't it?' A shiver ran up my spine as the thought I had been avoiding hammered home. I think I had known all along what had happened and who was responsible. 'Did you see him, Martha?'

'Didn't need to see him. Evil is like that. It reeks and leaves its stench like a cat out tomming and his stink is all over this. It's in this room and all around the cottage and there's only one way to get rid of it. If you don't, it's only a matter of time before it gets you.'

I no longer had any doubt Levi was in Launceston and the reason I'd seen him was because he had wanted me to know he was around. Like an animal toying with its prey, this was his modus operandi, the creation of fear in his victims until it smothered all rational thought.

Someone had betrayed me, for how else could he have found me?

My physical appearance had changed. I had lost a few kilos, changed my hair colour and style, replaced contacts with glasses and invested in a new wardrobe. It had cost, but worth every cent. Finding the right person to supply a new birth certificate and other documents had been more difficult for someone of my demographic with no links to the criminal world, but I had found the right person in the end.

Or had I?

It was always in the back of my mind that people who operated in this netherworld had no true loyalty to anyone once they had taken their money.

I was back where I had started. All of my efforts to begin a new life had been for nothing. However, where before there'd been fear and anxiety that led to paralysing panic attacks, now all I felt was a white hot anger. It wasn't that he had intended to kill me and killed an innocent person by mistake. It was that he had taken it as his divine right to take the life of another person and that, not content with victimising and hounding me for years and taking everything dear to me, he had now taken his need for revenge against imagined slights to a new level.

Martha hadn't taken her eyes off my face, as if reading my thoughts. 'You'll do nothing for the moment and I'll make sure he doesn't meet up with you until the time is right. You've still got unfinished business with Alice. Turn her from the path she's headed down and that will set us all free.'

'So you mean I should just sit here waiting until he decides to come for me?'

'He's scared himself off for the moment and left his little calling card as a reminder to you that he's still around. You know how he operates better than I do. It seems he doesn't mind too much how long it takes. The thrill for him is in the hunt. Killing Anna was an opportunistic error on his part. He saw her leave the cottage, thought it was you, and followed her up the steps. Not being as fit as she was, he had to really push himself to catch up with her. He blamed her for this and pushed her in the back in a fit of temper, only realising as she turned to look at him as the railing gave way that he had chased after the wrong person. Who knows whether he intended to kill or not? The fact is that he has and now he doesn't know if the police are after him or not. Let's not forget the level of paranoia that drives him. He came back to the cottage and left the card to keep the pressure on you, but I think he'll stay away until he's sure the police aren't after him and have finished their business here.'

This was the most words Martha had ever spoken without a break, usually content to keep her cryptic comments short.

'I'd go to the police, but they wouldn't believe me. That's something else he's made sure of.'

'The police will be speaking to him soon enough so don't you worry about it. Now, when are you seeing Alice again?'

'She's meant to be coming here in a couple of days, but now I'm not sure that's such a good idea. Not if people are still going to be hanging around, pointing out where it happened.'

'There's not much you can do about that. It's human nature. God knows I've seen enough of it over the years. The morbid curiosity of those who still live, I suppose.'

We talked a little longer, sharing sadness over needless loss of life, not only Anna, but of the many women who had taken refuge in the cottage. Martha explained her role as toll keeper that went beyond collecting coins at the gate, to keeping toll of the fatalities in the area, while saving those she could. A role she wanted me to take on with Alice to bring an end to this function of the cottage forever. I wasn't sure how this would work but I knew not to ask questions for which there are no answers, trusting after that we could both move on. In the meantime there was the police interview in town and then I intended to work steadily on making sense of the information I got from the library and trying to fit this with what I already had.

Elizabeth

I had been living at a lodging house and doing odd jobs for
the landlord after I got out of the invalid home three years
before. I liked a drink now and again. It numbed the misery
that had been the lot of so many of my counterparts sent out
for a crime so petty I'd forgotten what it was I was supposed
to have done. Life didn't get any easier with freedom either,
especially as I got older, for there was no pity for old women
in this colony. I had a reputation for being of dissipated habits
and often spent a week or two in the lock up, although I
wasn't always as drunk as I made out, using this as a ruse to
get a roof over my head and food in my belly.

In the end I just got fed up with the hand to mouth
existence. I was going on seventy five years and half crippled
with gout and I was tired of living. It seemed to me that if God
didn't want me then I'd just have to take myself to the devil.
Not that I believed in that stuff. You didn't live the life I had
and still have faith in anyone, mortal or otherwise.

I didn't take a drink that day, wanting to de sure I did it
properly and not slip in the shallow water before the real
event because I'd tried it once before and got a week's
imprisonment for my efforts.

I went down the back of the yacht club, out of sight of do
gooders. I tied my skirts down with string for modesty,
because even though I'd be dead and beyond earthly caring, I
wasn't about to display my old wares for the world to see.
Then I sort of launched myself into a roll towards the water.
The tide was up and deep at that point so it didn't take long

for the bubbles to stop.

I never found my way to either God or Satan and, while the fellowship of the cottage has been of some comfort, they're a restless lot and unease is all around me. If telling my story will get me out of here I'm happy to tell mine.

Chapter 18

Speaking with the police was not something I was comfortable doing. Not because I had anything to hide, unless I counted my recent encounters with Levi. But there was no way of proving his involvement with Anna's death, with only the word of a ghost to back up my story.

It had also been my experience their preferred version of any event would always be that from a practiced liar with scepticism shown to the truth teller. Martha counselled me to say only what I had known when speaking with them, anything beyond that would sound like an unbalanced rant.

An almost calm had descended on me in stages since my last meltdown in the cottage, as if I had disassociated from the person I had once been. The anxiety still nibbled around the edges, but I was somehow able to step aside from it before it took hold, to watch from a distance as a mother watches over a child, feeling the emotion but giving it room to manage independently. The medication helped, but this was something more than that, like an out of body experience in which I functioned better than I had for a long time. Today, it was something I consciously sought as I walked the couple of kilometres to the police station, not wanting to show nervousness or falter during the interview.

I had huge trust issues and police were a part of this. Some people couldn't see past the uniform or the role they professed to play in protecting communities. My experience showed they were just as vulnerable to stuffing up as the next person and that a uniform or label didn't change the essence of a person and never could.

Environment also played a big part in determining the practices of a particular station. Good leadership usually led to good policing, however this was less often the case, as leaders came from the rank and file and they took their bad habits with them up the line. The brotherhood nurtured in the academy, that need to watch each other's backs in times of danger had the capacity to take on a deeper, more sinister, interpretation that rolled over into turning a blind eye to poor work practice, corruption, and dishonesty in every form.

Successive governments had tried to clean up their police forces, with a few officers offered up as sacrificial lambs to take the heat off, however, the toxicity defied experimental antidotes and nothing ever changed.

Levi had been a part of this system of privilege, that place of never speaking out as insurance against the day it may need to be reciprocated. When his time came to call in the favours, it paid off handsomely, his out of control and unethical behaviour unchecked as he created havoc and an atmosphere of fear amongst those he targeted for his hate.

From the highest checkpoint of the department, the covering up and denial of his actions was resolute. That his personality disorder hadn't been identified at any stage of the selection process into the force or during the extensive training period, led me to wonder just how many others were administering the law according to their own warped view of life and sense of entitlement.

Experience had made me cautious and I had learnt to avoid any contact with police where possible and to say as little as I could get away with if such contact was unavoidable. The less I said meant the less chance of misinterpretation, deliberate or otherwise. I had also learnt to carefully read any statement before signing. The average person would be amazed at the difference an omission or addition of a couple words could make to any witness account or record of interview, or how, in the event of a dispute, the word of a police officer will be believed in court above that of an everyday citizen as if a title gave them immunity from questioning.

With this level of wariness on my part the interview was restrained, reiterating the information I had given the day. I was asked about my shoes, although they didn't elaborate on this, apart from suggesting they may want to look at the shoes I'd been wearing the day Anna met her death. I had the feeling it was all part of the process in preparing a report for the coroner and they were expecting a finding of accidental death, or whatever the specific terminology was for this. For her family this would be the best outcome. No long wait for a trial and the possibility of a not guilty plea to draw it out with subsequent appeals, and no wondering why someone had killed her, when any answer would never be enough. Better to get on with their grieving without these impediments. There'd be an inquest, with possible recommendation about maintenance of the track and replacement of old railings and that would be that.

I was out of the police station by twelve, as the sun was trying to break through the thunderclouds in their slow rumble across the sky. I hoped this was a sign the weather had turned. I didn't mind rain in moderation, but day after day of heavy downpours was enough to wipe even the most resilient smile off anyone's face.

The cottage had lost its appeal for me, so I took the sliver of sunshine as an omen to stay out longer and explore parts of the town I hadn't yet seen. I didn't have a camera with me, but my phone worked just as well for those spur of the moment shots and was less obtrusive in crowds. Some people got funny as soon as they saw a camera, conjuring an invasion of privacy scenario where no such intention existed. A phone camera was safer, no one taking any notice these days of a person with a device against their ear, in the hand with thumb flicking furiously over a miniature keypad, or held above the head while the owner searched for a signal from a less powerful network.

Heading straight up Charles Street, I bypassed the shopping precinct, detouring through Princes Square with its formal layout and central fountain, heading for an eatery in the high part of town. I wanted time alone, away from anything associated with the cottage but it wasn't that easy to escape reminders.

Looking out the west-facing window of the café, *The Arches* school dominated the hill. The grand Victorian mansion would never have been a shrinking violet. On display from so many angles, it stood as a constant reminder of its function as a maternity home in the days of harsher social judgement. It may have been a beacon of hope for some, but my research had shown it was a hope destined for despair, with the generational effect still felt today in the children and grandchildren of the lost ones.

I changed chairs to look out on the streetscape, taking random snaps as I waited for my order, always on the lookout for new angles, whether it was in writing or images, thinking ahead to the marriage between the two. I had written a lot about the immediate cataract area and the north side of the gorge, but I hadn't explored possibilities beyond that. The light and shadows cast a warmer, more welcoming glow on the rooftops on this side and I used this to sweep away the issues I had intended to muse upon. I was sorry I hadn't found my way to this spot earlier in the residence instead of confining myself to the cottage and surrounds. Fortified and refreshed, I began the downhill walk with cheerful optimism I'd be able to speak with Alice in a way she could make up her own mind about *Stony Rise* and the tragedy that had befallen her grandmother and mother. I had no intention of projecting my thoughts and opinions on to her, rather I would present her with facts and trust her intelligence and ability to form her own understanding of the past, without influence from another party. This was the benefit of well-rounded research. Make certain each point could be cross referenced from reliable sources, take away assumption and conjecture, look at the evidence objectively and without emotion and the truth would offer itself for consideration.

I didn't know how this fitted with the checks and balances of Martha's tally card. I didn't need to know. It crossed my mind that if there was only one more person to save, and if Martha had deemed that person to be Alice, then Anna's death would have increased the debit column and two lives needed to be saved before Martha and the women and children could move on. There was much I didn't understand. I thought back to past conversations we'd had, but she'd spoken in riddles most of the time and not answered any of my questions.

Coming down into the part where the sun rarely reached, the now familiar oppression returned and I wondered, not for the first time, what the mental health statistics were in the winter shadows of this place. Certainly the suicide rate for the period I had studied seemed abnormally high for a town of its size.

And poor Anna.

What had she done to deserve her fate other than befriend me?

The slow burning anger I felt toward Levi returned, and I forgot the chill of the streets as I contemplated an end to his tyranny.

I stopped at the toll house on my way home, drawn to it through curiosity about past keepers more than any real interest. Jana had offered me the key if I wanted to use it for any residency related activity and had the weather been warmer, I may have accepted the offer, but it held little appeal for me in this cold.

Peering through the windows to the narrow confines of its interior, where Martha and others like her had collected the tolls from sightseers and pleasure seekers, I could see only the tedium that accompanied the task. I traced my hand along the side of the booth and the door gave slightly, as if the catch was loose, however, when I pulled on the handle it opened freely.

Opening the narrow door further I saw a battered sports bag crammed into the space under the narrow counter and I was tempted to look inside.

If it had been there yesterday why hadn't the police found it and taken it away?

Instinct told me it was connected to Levi and I knew if I looked inside I'd find tools used in housebreaking, not the jemmy bar of old style breakers, but more sophisticated master keys available over the internet to those who knew what to look for. Levi had used similar to these to gain entry to my home and others, to find information useful to him and to plant listening devices. He wouldn't want to carry this lot around in case he was pulled up for a random search. He may have been a police officer in Victoria once, but he wasn't part of the brotherhood in this state.

I pulled the door to and left quickly. If Levi was watching, I didn't want him to think I was on to him. My finding left me feeling strangely exhilarated, like a marathon runner sighting the end flag.

Isabella

Sometimes in life you reach a point where it doesn't matter which road you choose, the destination will remain the same and that was the situation I found myself in that fateful Sunday. My mistress had only recently noticed my condition and berated me cruelly at every opportunity, comparing me to the girls in the bad houses. This was due in part to the gossip others made up about me being on the streets late at night and I went for a walk that Sunday to gather my thoughts about how to deal with my situation. I was deep in thought, but I would hardly call it melancholic as stated at the inquest. My aunt had also been on at me about the gossip and I set out for church, hoping to find some solace there. I felt unwell and went to the water's edge to dampen my handkerchief to apply as a compress when I was overcome by a stabbing pain in my side that caused me to lose my balance. The tide was full and the weight of my skirts dragged me under. I didn't mean to die and I could never commit such a sin as killing my own baby, however hard life might be. Once the truth be told my soul will be free.

Chapter 19

The table was set out with files and papers long before Alice was due to arrive. I had moved the desk back to its original position, no longer concerned whether I was being watched or not. I used the waiting time to catch up on my social media pages, writing a blog post about nothing in particular, reading comments and replying where appropriate.

Nothing from Levi that I could detect.

I clenched my teeth at the thought of him, of Anna's helplessness when he came upon her from behind, leaving her little chance to defend herself. Even if she had it would have been futile because, what he lacked in height, he made up for in brute strength.

What a hideous death.

The police had said she had died instantly, although I had my doubts, imagining her terrible struggle for breath as her air supply diminished. It didn't bear thinking about and I was glad to have my thoughts interrupted by the knock at the door.

Alice was keen to have a look at the cottage and it was important she feel, if not at home, then at least comfortable in this house that overlooked the place where her grandmother and mother met their deaths.

'It's very small, isn't it?'

'Yes, it is, big enough for the purpose of residencies, but hard to visualise a family living in this space.'

'Pretty spooky, too,' she said as she entered the bedroom, the darkest area of the cottage, 'look, I've got goose bumps,' she lifted her arm as a gesture, leaving her sleeve down, 'do you think it's haunted?'

'Do you?' I was beginning to sound like Martha, 'but yes, I do think there's something here. Energy left over from the past or something like that. It's also always cold on this side of the cottage so that may account for the goose bumps.'

'Maybe.' She seemed keen to discount the obvious, 'Have you seen anything, anyone?'

'That's an odd question.'

'No it's not,' the snappy Alice returned, 'not when that's what we're talking about.'

'In an old house like this, one of such social historical significance, it would be easy to imagine anything when things go bump in the night.' I laughed, wanting to make light of the turn of conversation.

'I suppose so,' she looked straight at me, 'I believe in spirits you know. I've seen things.'

'I'm sure you have. All writers do. It's where our stories come from isn't it?'

'I'm serious.'

'I know you are, Alice.'

We were back in the study now and I invited her to sit where we could share the table top, changing the focus to the purpose of the meeting.

She was most interested in my findings from the library and had no argument when these further validated the information we had looked at previously. It had been my intention to stay away from the subject of Graeme Rogel unless Alice raised it. She did, although not in the way I'd been expecting.

'You know I think you might be right about that Graeme dude. After our last meeting I spent hours and hours googling adoption related pages and looking up every reference I could find and almost every website, in Australia at least, is of his creation. Most of it is just a cut and paste job of what he's posted elsewhere, but even I can see how he's used these to give himself credibility. I think there are probably lots of people who are so desperate for answers they just don't see the similarities between the sites,' she laughed, 'his poor spelling and use of grammar give it away. He's a real try hard.'

'I agree and I also believe many people have been hurt by his assertions.'

'It's probably his social media pages that tell more about who he really is and I was shocked at how abusive he became whenever anyone tried to challenge his opinions, no matter how respectfully they did it. And I learnt a new word or terminology, micro-aggression, it seems that any person who has a different opinion than his, no matter how politely stated, is immediately accused of displaying micro-aggression.'

'Yes, I noticed that, too, seeing it as yet another control device. I could also see he purposefully provoked any person who held an opposing view and then screamed victim on his various adoptee web pages, accusing others of doing to him was he was actually doing himself. He's a complex and quite dangerous individual.'

'He did it to me, too. We'd written back and forth a bit as I'd told you, so when I read some of his comments I asked him why he didn't actually read what people had written instead of going off in a rant that was quite often off topic. I didn't actually say that last bit though, just asked the question, friendly like.' She told the story slowly, considering each word as if, in telling it now, she was also processing what had happened. 'I was shocked, really shocked, by his reply. He started out telling me I'd been brainwashed by the other side, whoever the other side is supposed to be, and when I attempted to clarify this he lost it completely, calling me names and trying to put me down.'

'I'm sorry that had to happen to you, Alice. There are people in this world who are mentally unwell, but most don't carry on like he does. Some do,' Levi was never far from my thoughts, 'and it's people like us who bear the brunt of the behaviour that comes from their poor judgement.'

'Oh, I can take it, I've heard worse. I don't know how he's got away with it though. Sometimes I wonder about Facebook and what people get away with. What he says about other people is pure slander.'

'Yes it is. Unfortunately, some of the people he talks about are no longer living, so it's the good name of these people he seeks to tarnish, people who have no way of defending the reputations they earned from a lifetime of good work.'

'But that's just awful.'

'I know, but who'd take him on? I know I wouldn't. I know danger when I see it.'

'It's not fair though, is it?'

'No, it's not.'

'I can see what he does though. He develops a theory about something and then bends the facts to fit. And I can see something else, too. I think he can't accept that his mother gave him up for adoption and needs to make her helpless or powerless in that decision to a point he can live with it.'

'That's a clever observation, Alice.'

'I've taken psychology the last two years but, more than that, I've been able to see something of my mother, and myself, too, if I'm to be totally honest, in his behaviour. One of the things my mother could never come to terms with was that she had been adopted, given away by her own mother, and it ate away at her until there was nothing left. She didn't hit out at other people like he does, she was too fragile for that, but she punished herself for her perceived unlovability, if that's a word. All she ever wanted was to find her mother and when she found out she'd been dead all the years of her searching it was too much for her to live with,' she looked out the window, 'she went into the river just over there, you know.'

'I did know, yes.'

'And I think my grandmother went in pretty much the same spot.'

I nodded that I was listening and understood the gravity.

'I've thought about it too, you know. Killing myself, that is. I used to cut myself when I was younger. Stupid, eh?'

'Dangerous perhaps. Stupid, no. Most people who self-harm are usually trying to deal with an even deeper emotional pain and use this as a way of coping. You've obviously learnt to understand it and some of those deeper issues.'

'As much as one can, I suppose.'

We continued working through the papers, the history of *Stony Rise* and various aspects of legislation relating to adoption, with Alice underlining and highlighting sections she wanted to read more fully later.

'Have you thought what you might do with all this information?'

'I have, and I have Graeme to thank for that.'

'How's that?'

'Someone has to tell the story of *Stony Rise*, the good the bad and the ugly of it. It's an important part of the social history of Launceston and Australia in general and it's a vital part of my own history. I can whinge and moan all I like about my life or I can do something about it. I can't change what happened to my grandmother or my mother, but I can at least tell their story. Not by pointing the finger and crying foul, but by careful research, using what you've given me as a base for this, and writing the story objectively.' Alice could be blunt to a point of rudeness at times, but there was no disputing her maturity in other areas. She showed a common sense many could take an example from.

'Sounds promising.'

'I've already written a short history of the school as you know, but I realise now I've put too much emotion into it, too much of myself, and I need to step back and revise this so other people will want to read it.'

'Will that be combined with the other story?'

'No, I don't think so. I want to explore the paranormal activity in the school and that would detract from the human element of the other, I think. Either way, I'm taking time out to complete my studies. Once I've finished uni then I'll dust them off and look at them again from a new perspective. Who knows, I may even apply for a residency at the cottage. ' She smiled and this time it reached her eyes softening her face to show her vulnerability.

'That would be great and your plan is sound. If there's any way I can help you I'd be glad to.'

'You've already helped me, more than you know. All this,' she tapped the table, 'has given me a sense of direction, and if you hadn't given me the links for Graeme I might just as easily ended up as twisted and resentful as he is. It was like looking into the mirror of the future and seeing what I'd look like if I'd continued to feed my bitterness. I sort of feel sorry for him but I also think he's a bastard,' she looked at me with that direct way she had, 'and I mean that. He might have been born a bastard, but it's his choice whether he acts like one.'

I had to agree with her on every count and we chatted as we packed the papers and files into Alice's bag about her plans to study journalism at university to following year. She wanted to be a teller of truth, but her true vocation was to be a writer and her journey in that direction had already begun.

If this was what Martha meant by keeping Alice safe I believed this had been done, however, I watched her after she left, the cottage following her movements across the bridge and round the corner into Paterson Street, before I was satisfied she was also safe from Levi.

Anna

I'd always had a premonition that my death would be associated with this area that had been central to my life, yet this knowledge couldn't save me in the end. Nothing could have saved me.

I found the cataract precinct a place of dark menace that repelled and enticed at the same time. It called to me and I came running, buying the house at the top of the hill as if that somehow gave me control over the inevitable. I ran its paths each day in defiance of the pervasive reminder of past tragedies, ignoring invitations at every turn to take my own leap into the belly of the restless serpent. That's why I ran so fast, to outpace whispered temptation and to deny the presentiment of my own death.

I had the gift of clairvoyance they said, passed down the maternal line from my mother and her mother before her, although it was a gift I had never wanted and one I sought to repudiate whenever the knowing came to me. To me it was a curse. I didn't want to know about the present, past or future of others or the lurid details of their lives. I fought the knowledge, denying it entry into rational thought, yet it still had a habit of seeping through the cracks when I wasn't expecting it. Worse still had been the visitations, the phantasmal presences around the river banks and paths that rustled the grass and called in the wind as I passed, 'Anna, Anna...'

And nowhere had these manifestations been stronger than in the cottage, where they gathered en masse in the kitchen and clustered at darkened windows, pale faces and dripping hair, the forgotten souls of the three rivers.

I didn't trust Martha either, holding her responsible for the situation at the cottage, for encouraging women and children to her hearth when she could have been guiding them to their rest.

The first time I met Francesca I recognized she, too, had the gift of knowing and had some form of clairvoyance of which she'd probably not even been aware. That's why I never questioned her about the cottage and why I never warned her that Levi was about. It had been too complex to explain and I had hoped that in offering friendship she'd confide in me if she needed to. I sensed her vulnerability and wanted to protect her if I could and, in the end, I protected her in a way I had never anticipated.

Chapter 20

As much as I wanted to see Levi brought to justice for killing Anna, I had no way of proving he had even been in the area that day. I hadn't seen him. Martha had, but I couldn't see her as a credible police witness, even if she had been able to come forward. The time was approaching when the next part of her plan had to be put into action. There was danger in Levi's unpredictability, however, as long as I kept a clear mind all should be well, for me anyway.

As my time in the cottage drew to a close I spent more time with Martha as she checked and rechecked the progress I made on the women's' stories, making sure every date was correct, every detail precise. She had promised the women their truth would be told, that they'd all be leaving once this was complete, each going to where they should have been long ago.

The cottage would no longer require a caretaker, its purpose complete. This hadn't been as straight forward as I had hoped, with many interruptions and wavering from the women themselves, some afraid to cross over, others so caught in the limbo between life and death they believed they still belonged with the living. And they worried about the children, if they'd be separated and who'd look after those whose mothers had already gone. I didn't have the answers and relied on Martha to ease their concerns. I was just a writer who'd found myself conversing with the dead.

Whether Martha thought her leaving would bring an end to the deaths at the cataract I didn't know. My research had shown the river deaths had decreased over the years, although this didn't mean there was less sadness and unfairness in the world, if anything there was probably more. The decrease could be attributed to a more enlightened society and an improved understanding and service response for mental health issues although, as I had found out to my disadvantage, there were many, such as Levi, who continued to fall through the cracks.

The residency had been good for me in a number of ways. I still experienced panic attacks, but I was learning slowly how to check these before they became fully debilitating. Sometimes this seemed easier than others. I had also become less fearful of Levi since Anna's death. This had been due in part to the anger I felt at what he had done to so many lives, to my life and the taking of Anna's and all because of imagined slights against him. As if he had some god given right to act as judge and jury in the kangaroo court of his mind and dispense justice as he saw fit.

I understood mental illness as much as any person standing on the outside looking in was able to. What I didn't understand was how he had slipped through so many opportunities for intervention. His behaviour during adolescence that should have alerted his parents or teachers had gone unchecked, and his inability to complete his first round of training at the police academy due to an emotional breakdown should have rung alarm bells and yet somehow they let him through for a second time. The growing recklessness I felt in regard to Levi I attributed to Martha assurances, trusting her to keep me informed and safe.

It had only been on reflection that I could see the parallels between Alice and I. Age aside, we were both embarking on a writing project about other people, other women, who lived in another time. Hers was more personal, while mine was about women of no relation to me. The common theme between the two stories was in the setting of the cataract and the circumstance of death. The difference was she had chosen her subject while mine had chosen me.

My last days in the cottage were marred by Anna's death and the guilt I felt, knowing it should have been me and knowing who the perpetrator was without speaking up. It didn't matter how I justified this, responsibility was a heavy weight.

Throughout most of the residency I had struggled to find any sense of peace in the cottage, finding it oppressive with a restlessness that came with an overfill of the past. While this had in no way impeded my work, if anything I had produced more and of a greater depth and quality than I had thought possible, I would have preferred this to have been in a more psychologically comfortable environment. And although fear was something I had lived with as an extension of my life, I had hoped my stay in the cottage would give some respite from this. Instead it had added to it, with hauntings and poltergeist activity I hadn't understood, and the returning menace of Levi, so I couldn't understand why I had a sudden sense of attachment and an almost reluctance to be leaving.

The evening before my departure was almost celebratory, sharing it with Martha and the women and children, all preparing to leave at the same time. Martha had outlined the plan to me so there'd be no error when the time came. Most important to her was placement of the manuscript holding the stories of the women of the cataract. She insisted it be left on the desk by my laptop where I wouldn't forget it. This didn't make a lot of sense to me and I argued it would be better to put it with all my papers packed in the holdall near the door, but she would have none of this and I passed it off as something she had used to pacify the women, to show them the story had at least been written and ready to submit to a publisher.

She instructed me to make contact with Levi and arrange to meet him early in the morning, before joggers began their routine run along the path to the cliff grounds. She'd be waiting in the shadows and take care of the rest. He would meet his end in the flooded river, with no blood on my hands or conscience, and I'd make my way back to the cottage, collect my belongings and be on my way back to the mainland.

To say I had been nervous about contacting him was an understatement. I was petrified. I also didn't think he'd buy it. Why would he when I had gone to the lengths I had to get away from him? Surely someone with his level of paranoia would be suspicious if I contacted him out of the blue. I argued this back and forth with Martha. but she remained unmoving.

'He'll turn up. He won't be able to help himself.'

'You don't understand how terrified of him I am.' My earlier feelings of bravado had deserted me now the meeting was imminent.

'I think I have a fair idea. I've lived with you these past weeks haven't I? Either you want to be shod of him or you don't,' she feigned indifference with a shrug of her shoulders, but the tone of her voice said otherwise, 'it's your life.'

'But...'

'You know I always thought you were made of stronger stuff than this, but you're not much different to that lot in there,' she cocked her head toward the kitchen, 'cowards the lot of them.'

There was no answer to this. I knew I was being manipulated and had to accept this was to my advantage. Unless I took action, I'd spend the rest of my life looking over my shoulder and jumping at shadows, waiting for that fearful unknown.

Too afraid to hear his voice in case it paralysed me into inaction, I opted for a text message, turning the phone off as soon as I pressed send. I neither wanted nor needed a reply. The minute I sent the text, I set out for the appointed meeting place, allowing time to position myself as Martha had directed. I hadn't seen her that morning, but this was her plan and I knew she'd be ready to play her part.

My hands were shaking with more than cold as I hurried up the pathway, the torch casting a zig zag arc of light as I rushed through the dark. With more rain overnight the river was higher than before, tumbling furiously from the rapids and lashing the slate grey sentinels of time. I shivered to think of the lives lost in this place, those sacrificed as a life not worth living and others taken on the whim of someone else. In a short while it would be Levi's turn, his body tossing and spinning and running with the current. I couldn't let myself think of this as unlawful, translating it instead to a symbolic ending of all he had put me through.

From my vantage point at the suggested meeting place I had a clear view of the approach from the town side, from which direction I assumed he'd be coming, my eyes catching every movement as the sky lightened; the heave of a branch, the flip of a leaf. I thought I caught a glimpse of Martha's dress whipping from between a long crevice in the cliff and hoped Levi wasn't able to see it and realise he was about to step into a trap. If he turned and ran now, the whole plan would be over and I'd be left forever at his mercy.

Then I saw him, lumbering in that way he had, unhurried, appearing unfazed. It was part of his menace. I tried to stay calm, to ignore the racing of my heart and the urge to run on legs that threatened to give way. I had to steel myself to hold my ground, to stand where I had been instructed to maximise the element of surprise when Martha appeared, to make sure he never saw her coming or knew what hit him as he tumbled through the railing loosened for the purpose.

When Martha had talked about throwing him over the railing I knew this would never work, as neither she nor I had the strength to do this either singly or together. He was too simply too heavy and had the strength of his years. The whole plan looked like unravelling, until she came up with the idea of loosening the railing. She said it had been the manner of Anna's death that had given her the idea, a sort of poetic justice, and I agreed.

Neither Levi nor I spoke as he came nearer, until he was almost at the meeting point. I locked eyes with him and said the words Martha had told me to say, although with less confidence than she had suggested.

'I know what you did to Anna, you murdering creep.'

Even with the anger I felt toward him I couldn't speak without a tremor in my voice. Knowing this could give him the upper hand I resolved to say nothing further, relying instead in the direct eye contact I knew he hated.

He lurched forward and I stepped to the side as I had been instructed to place him near to the railing, when Martha rushed across the path to complete the plan. Then there was a rush of movement as Levi grabbed me by the throat and pushed me back. I felt the give of the iron rail as it jerked free and the outward fall over the rapids, then the sensation of falling faster and faster until I became as one with the river.

The last thing I saw before the brown water filled my eyes was the image of Martha standing at the edge of the path and behind her the women and children of the cataract, fading into the morning mist.

Francesca

The cottage was quiet when I woke, a fire burning in the old wood stove and the kettle bubbling away on top and I knew I was on my own. And it continued this way for a long time. Nobody seemed to want to stay in the cottage the first couple of years after my death.

My novel, the true purpose of my residency at the cottage was never completed beyond manuscript form.

The Women of the Cataract manuscript had been found and published by the council as I had originally hoped it would be, although I had expected to be around to see this happen. It received mixed reviews, however, it had been deemed to have social history merit and won a number of literary prizes. A copy sits on the bookshelf in the study, a grim reminder to any visiting artist of the darker side of the cottage.

It's peaceful here most of the time, except when visitors come to stay, the writers and artists with their creative minds and interpretive ideas, and then I keep to myself. In between times I rest and enjoy the peace I had always longed for, although I'm getting tired of my own company. There's not a lot of traffic treading the path from life to death around the rivers these days, the toll in my time standing at nil.

I suppose one day I'll find someone to take my place as caretaker, but not for a while, it depends on who I have to share the place with. Alice will be back someday soon to complete her work on *Stony Rise* and its links to the cataract and I look forward to helping her. Who knows, as an investigative journalist, she may have an interest in writing the truth about my death and finally bring Levi to justice. She may even have the attributes required for the position of caretaker.

Francesca